JAZZ AND ELLA

A Mouse Gate Adventure

Jeffrey Lovell

TotalRecall Publications, Inc.

TotalRecall Publications, Inc.
1103 Middlecreek
Friendswood, Texas 77546
281-992-3131 281-482-5390 Fax
www.totalrecallpress.com

Printed in the United States of America with simultaneous printings in Australia, Canada, and United Kingdom.

FIRST EDITION
1 2 3 4 5 6 7 8 9 10

To Laurie Rossi of Fairview, New Mexico, a colleague for many years and the editor of all my books. No one knows grammar and syntax better than she and she's been invaluable to me as a friend and expert.

Award Winning Author

 is a native Chicagoan, with 3 degrees from the University of Illinois and an earned doctorate from Vanderbilt University. Jeff taught high school writing and literature for thirty three years and sponsored the school paper, Student Council and several other activities. He ran the drama program at two high schools, teaching and directing and designing sets, lighting and costumes. His specialty in his career focused on Shakespeare. Since he retired from education, Jeff has served as a theatre and film critic for a television station and appears frequently to review theatre and literature.

Introduction

Orlando Adventure tells the story of Jazz, a fourteen year old high school freshman, and his best friend, Ella, who meet on the way to Disney World. A supernatural being gives them each a magic amulet, which the children use to transport themselves to new and different worlds. They meet and deal many situations that cause them to face their fears and even terrors; that suggest ways that situations can be handled; and they see some of the choices that they will have to confront as they grow up.

CHAPTER 1

Jazz sat on an airplane seat looking out the window at the Tarmac below him, waiting for the big jet to take off. He was sitting by himself on this trip. Mom sat across the aisle from him, nodding to him from time to time. A large, rather handsome man sat next to her, and he leaned forward and waved to Jazz, giving him a broad smile.

Mom seemed to know the man, and to like him. There hadn't been time for introductions, since the man and a girl came on board just before the plane doors closed. Then it was 'Fasten Your Seatbelts', pull your chairs up, and all the instructions flight attendants always give.

Jazz knew he ought to be excited, and really, this vacation to Disney World sounded terrific. Still he had to struggle to act like this was really going to be a lot of fun since he probably would be pretty much alone with no other kids to join him running around the the parks. His stomach hurt most of the time, but he tried not to talk about it much. He knew when he did his mom would get into her "examination mode" and take his temperature and look down his throat, and all that.

Mom knew what to look for in terms of body pain. She'd become a famous doctor, after all—like, really famous. She worked at a large teaching hospital, and she was a very good doctor. People from all over their area came to see her in her specialty, Internal Medicine.

Everyone *told* him how good she was, anyhow. When he got sick, and he didn't get sick often, she always knew just who to take him to, who to consult and what medicines to give him.

That was the worst part. A lot of the medicine he took tasted so bad, and made him sleepy, or feel even sicker but he tried not to worry Mom.

Sitting alone on the plane, Jazz closed his eyes and his thoughts wandered back to the time of 'THE DIVORCE'. Jazz remembered every moment of it as if it was yesterday. Mom and Dad hadn't gotten along for months, ever since Mom learned that Dad had been dating another woman.

One day they invited him downstairs for a talk. Except Mom and Dad weren't talking. They were yelling. He'd never heard such language in their house. Yeah, at school and in the neighborhood, some kids used real nasty language. Sometimes they even directed it at Jazz; like they wanted him to fight them.

Jazz could take care of himself, but he didn't like fighting. Running races, playing ball, all those things—yeah, Jazz was good at those things. He was usually the first one picked for baseball games, and he'd been playing ball with the older kids for a long time— since he was five. He was faster than most of the other kids, too, even the older ones. He'd done well in Youth Football, in sixth and seventh and even eighth grade.

But then, when he was just eight, he found himself face up against something he couldn't handle. Mom and Dad told Jazz they wouldn't be living together anymore.

The next day, Jazz did go to school. That's when the stomach aches started. Mom made him go and said they had to go on with their lives as if nothing happened.

He thought about another time when he found himself having to pretend as if everything was okay. He remembered going over to Willie's house, his neighbor and friend. Willie was watching what he called a Zombie movie about people who looked pretty disgusting with grey wrinkly faces, hollow eyes, and they were walking around after they were dead. Jazz had never liked scary movies at all, especially when he was eight. Some of the kids had called him a baby because of it, but he never saw any reason to be scared if you didn't have to be. So he managed to pretend that the movie had been really cool.

This time, though, the pretending didn't work very well. Mr. Urich, his P. E. teacher, asked him to stay after class that first day and said something about how Jazz didn't look like himself, and was everything okay? Jazz, very embarrassed, started to cry and told him that his parents were getting a divorce. Mr. Urich didn't look shocked at all. Neither did Mr. Plecas, the principal, when Mr. Urich took Jazz in to see him.

"Look, Jazz," said Mr. Plecas, who had always been nice to him. "You don't have to be ashamed of crying about that. Not at all. Remember when Randy Newland fell on the playground and broke his arm?"

Jazz did remember. The arm had snapped in two, and the break looked like it hurt like crazy. Randy had been screaming, Jazz recalled, and not just with pain, but with profound fear. Jazz thought of how Randy kept saying "I can't believe it. I just can't believe it."

Jazz nodded to Mr. Plecas and Mr. Urich, and Mr. Plecas put his arm on Jazz's shoulder to comfort him. "Look," said Mr. Plecas. "What happened to you is just as bad as what happened to Randy. I'm serious."

"What do you mean?" asked Jazz.

"I lost my dad when I was your age," said Mr. Plecas. "We went on a vacation as a family and he drowned in a lake up in Minnesota. When I found out I ran and hid in the woods. They couldn't find me for a couple of hours. My mom had to take care of the family all by herself after that."

Jazz started to cry again, and his pain now included feeling really sorry for Mr. Plecas and not just himself.

Mr. Plecas let him sit in the office by himself until after lunch. Jazz began to feel kind of numb and his stomach was hurting again, but he went back to class, not talking, just doing the work of writing and reading, trying not to think about going home and facing the house without his dad.

At last, though, he had to get on the bus and go back to his house out in the country. He got off the bus at his stop and walked home—about a half mile, Dad had once told him.

Once he got home, Jazz realized he was hungry. He hadn't eaten much of his lunch. He poured a glass of juice, and then fixed a peanut butter and raw honey sandwich. Once he ate, he did feel better, and decided to check out the house.

Everything looked the same as ever except for his parents' room. Dad had the closet opposite the end of the huge king size bed with the big canopy over it. The door stood open, and Jazz could see that Dad had emptied out the closet. The drawers Dad had always used were pulled out part way, and Jazz walked over to see that Dad's underwear drawer, socks drawers, and even the drawer that Dad hadn't allowed Jazz to look into had all been emptied.

Jazz sat down on what had been his Dad's side of the bed and tried hard not to cry again.

His mother found him lying on the bed sometime later when she came home from her medical office. Jazz remembered he had fallen into a deep sleep and had scary dreams of walking dead people, but he couldn't remember anything else about the dreams that had seemed so frightening at the time.

Mom took Jazz out to dinner that night and they drove to one of their favorite places for pizza, a rare treat. They even ordered soda pop and went out for some ice cream afterward at a Baskin Robbins. As they ate, Jazz kept thinking of the word 'bribe', but he wasn't sure what it meant: something like maybe paying someone to do something you want him to.

That night, eight year old Jazz climbed into the bath tub and lingered in the hot water longer than he usually did. He played with some tub toys, something he never did anymore and which he didn't want anyone to know about, because the other kids would really tease him about it. It just felt good to sit in the hot water and think of something other than all the yucky stuff swirling around him in real life.

That night, Mom came to his bedroom and made sure, as always, that he was tucked in. Of course, tonight Dad didn't come. This was the first time Dad had not come in to kiss him goodnight as long as Jazz could remember.

"Dear little Jazz Hands," Mom said. "I know you're heartbroken. I probably should have let you stay home. But I didn't have anyone to stay with you, and I thought you might feel better if you picked up your life and went on as soon as you can." Jazz nodded. "Jazzy," said Mom. "We just have to make it through one day at a time, okay?"

Jazz mumbled 'okay,' or something, and clutched his stomach.

That had all happened a number of years ago. The next day had been about as bad as the first. So had the next. The next week hadn't been too bad, except when a big eighth grader, one of the school bullies, had decided to pick him as his daily target and shoved him into a locker. Mom had told him to be brave and Dad, when he finally did come to see him—about a month after he'd moved out—had told him the same thing. Jazz never could understand why his Dad didn't want to see him more often. Jazz wanted to see him all the time and just decided he must have done something really wrong.

Finally, several weeks, and then a whole bunch of months, and then a few years, had gone by.

Then, at Christmas Eve last year, he got into bed, his stomach still hurting him as it always did at night. His mom came in, as she always did, to say goodnight. The fact that he had grown older did not alter this evening habit.

"Jazz," said Mom. "I've been thinking we should go to Florida. I think maybe a vacation to visit Mickey is just what we need! How does that sound? I've planned our trip so we leave about a month from now." Jazz, for the first time in a while, began to get excited. Everyone he knew would give anything to go to Disneyworld . He and his mom hadn't taken a vacation for a long time. It might be good to go away. But then the thought of the possibility of loneliness started to overwhelm him.

"Sure it's okay," said Jazz. "That'd be great. We haven't been there since—"

He bit off the rest of the sentence, as the pain of not having his dad come with him struck. When they went on trips or vacations before the divorce, it'd just be the three of them and Jazz treasured the memories from those vacations. He even remembered the first night when he'd ordered chocolate milk.

He didn't have to finish the sentence. Mom knew what he meant. Mom said goodnight, reminded Jazz not to forget to pray, and Jazz tried to go to sleep.

The next month had dragged by, as Jazz and his mom prepared for their trip to Florida. He was going to miss a few days of school, but Mr. Plecas, the school principal, had grinned and told him not to worry. He asked Jazz to try to do some school work while he was there and said the rest of the school envied him getting to go to Disney.

Jazz wasn't very concerned about how the rest of the school felt about him. He was a pretty good athlete, though not the fastest, and a pretty good student, though not the best. A girl whom Jazz didn't know, except by sight, was the best, far and away. He had never really talked to her and was pretty sure she didn't know him. At least, she never greeted him in the hall.

To tell the truth, Jazz rather enjoyed being a loner. He didn't like the so-called popular kids in the eighth and seventh grades, who walked around in exclusive groups and didn't let anyone join their cliques. He had a couple of friends he ate lunch with, and then he went home where he'd play on the internet a little, but generally, he like to read.

So as he sat by himself on the airplane, he felt rather at home—by himself, reading a book while listening to his favorite band, the Newsboys, on his headphones.

He felt a nudge, and turned to look at whom it was. To his surprise, the girl from his school who got such great grades stood there, with her hair in braids and wearing a cute, sporty-looking dress. He pulled off his head phones and looked up.

"Hi," said the girl. "I'm Ella. Can I sit with you?"

Jazz was so surprised he could hardly talk. "Well—uh—sure," he said. He'd been sitting on the aisle, and now put the armrest up so he could slide across to the window seat. Now he recognized her as the girl who'd almost missed the flight and had come onto the plane with Mom's—er—friend.

"You go to Harrison Junior High," said the girl, "in Wildwood. I've seen you."

"Yeah, I do," said Jazz, who realized that he must sound like a fool. He suddenly didn't know where to put his hands. He wasn't sure if you were supposed to shake hands with girls or not. She solved his dilemma by putting out her right hand. He took it somewhat numbly.

She laughed a little. "Do you think you can tell me your name?" she laughed, amused by his obvious lack of social skills.

"Oh," he mumbled. "Well, people call me Jazz. Jazz O'Neill."

"Your name is Jazz?" she looked surprised.

"I know it's kind of unusual," he said. "It's a nickname. I'm really named Jasper."

"Really," she said. "That's unusual. I've never met anyone named Jasper."

"My mom is a doctor," said Jazz.

Ella looked at him. Jazz didn't continue.

"Er…" she began. "Should I see something I'm not?"

"Oh," he said. "Well, when she was in college, she got to be in a musical play called *The Music Man*. One of the songs has a line about something like 'an out of town Jasper'."

"Yeah, I think I've heard it," smiled Ella.

"You have?" said Jazz.

"Sure," said Ella. "My Dad likes musicals. He's always taken me to see high school and college musicals and plays. I know we've seen *The Music Man*."

"Does your mom go too?" asked Jazz.

Ella didn't say anything. Instead she became very quiet, her smile disappeared, and she looked down, staring at the hands that were now clenched in her lap. A few moments passed, while Jazz realized that she was about to cry.

"Did I—" he began. "Did I say something that hurt you?" he mumbled.

"You didn't know," she said. "It's okay."

"Didn't know what?" he asked.

"Didn't know my mom died," she said. "My mom died a couple years ago. She died of cancer. She found out in March and died in September. The doctors couldn't help her."

Jazz didn't know what to say. He'd never met someone whose mom was dead. He knew, though, that he felt terrible now. At least his dad was still alive even if he didn't see him as much as he wished.

"I'm sorry…" he tried, but then realized he'd probably said the wrong thing again.

Ella shook her head. A moment later, Jazz asked, "Can you tell me how you got your name?"

His new friend brightened, her wide smile returned, and she became very animated as she began to speak. "Sure," said Ella. "I'm named after a famous singer named Ella from a long time ago."

"That's kind of unusual too, I guess," he said. "I like it, though."

"Thank you," she said. "My Mom worked as a kind of a musician. She liked to sing, and she did it in night clubs before and after she married my Dad. She paid for college and graduate school doing her singing."

"Uh-huh," said Jazz. "I don't see…"

"Oh, yeah," said Ella. "Her favorite singer was Ella Fitzgerald. I've grown up listening to her music."

"I don't think I know about her," said Jazz. He thought that it was better to be honest than pretend to be aware of Ella Fitzgerald only for her to discover later he was lying to impress her.

"It's okay," she said. "I can play you some music on my iPad with Ella singing. Also, my dad has a bunch of old records he plays every once in a while."

This conversation came to an end and the two children sat in a rather awkward silence. Ella spoke at last.

"Where are you going in Florida?" she asked.

"Disney," he said. Then he thought that wasn't saying enough, and added, "I mean, Walt Disney World."

"I know," she said. "That's good, Jazz."

"Why?" he asked. "I mean, why do you care about it?"

"Because we're going there, too," she added. "Where are you going to stay?"

"I think Mom said something about The Contemp… er, The—Uh—"

"The Contemporary," she said. "It's a big hotel. It's really a neat place. The monorail goes right through the middle of the hotel. You just hop on it and you can get to Epcot or The Magic Kingdom in just a few minutes.

"Oh, yeah, that's it," he nodded.

"That's great," said his new friend. "We're going to stay there too."

"Oh!" said Jazz. "So I guess—" He hesitated. "Maybe we could do some things together?"

"Well, yeah," she grinned. "I hope we can do that. That would really be fun. I was wishing I had someone more my age to ride all the rides. I mean, my Dad is lots of fun and all, but...."

"I know what you mean", Jazz said, interrupting her. He opened his mouth to elaborate, but then, in the next second, everything in both of their lives changed forever.

CHAPTER 2

The seat in front of them abruptly swelled to twice its normal size. Then, to the amazement of both of them, it contracted and slid backward, changing its shape as it did. Now, as they watched, the chair became a golden throne.

Jazz gulped and wrenched his eyes away from the unbelievable thing that was happening in front of them to steal a glance at Ella. Her eyes had gone wide with surprise and even some fear as well. It occurred to him that was strange also. He realized that he thought this girl who'd just befriended him was fearless. They both returned their focus to the seat in front of them, unable to speak.

Now a large man—he seemed to be a man, but he was gold all over—sat on the throne in front of them.

"Jazz," he said. "Ella."

Neither Ella or Jazz could respond. "Speak," the huge gold man said. "Do not be afraid."

Ella found her voice. "We aren't afraid," she said, and he smiled and nodded.

"You are not indeed," he said. "You will agree that you're surprised?"

Now Jazz spoke up. "Yes, Sir," he said.

"Good," he nodded. "Always be honest with me."

"Yes, sir," they agreed.

"I came to you because you are both going to be called to an adventure," said the Man. "When you come to the ride at Disney called Space Mountain, we will meet again. I will take you away with me for what will seem to be a long time, but it will take no time in your world."

"Take us away?" said Jazz. "Take us where?"

"Do not be afraid," said the Man. "Eat and rest. Be at peace. Become fast friends. You will need to be able to trust one another. Can you do that?"

They glanced at one another and nodded at the same time.

"Please say it," he said, and his voice rumbled like thunder.

The teen-agers looked at each other again but they knew what he meant. "I promise," said Jazz, and Ella responded at the same time, "I promise."

"Excellent," said the Man. "Here are two gifts, on for each of you. Put them on these chains and hang them around your necks."

"What are they, Sir?" asked Ella.

"They are Amulets, and you can see the designs on them. They will allow you to see things, to go places, and to understand what others are saying. Do not lose them. They are ancient and invaluable."

The two teenagers looked at each other and said, "We promise."

The Golden man looked deeply into their eyes and, in the next instant, the seat in front of them looked like a seat again, the airplane appeared all around them, and Jazz and Ella realized that they were holding one another's hand.

They quickly let go, but each one could still feel the warmth of the other's hand. It had provided strength for them, feeling the presence of another person. "Oh, good," said a deep voice next to Ella in the aisle.

The two teenagers looked up into the face of a kind, handsome man. "Dad," said Ella. "This is—"

"Jazz," he said. "Yes, I know. Your mother has been telling me about you."

"She has?" said Jazz.

"Yes, indeed," said the man. "I sat down with her when my daughter came over to sit with you. We've been keeping each other company on this flight."

Jazz and Ella exchanged glances and smiled at one another.

"What happened to you?" asked the man.

"What do you mean?" asked Ella.

"We were watching you and you both got really quiet and stared straight ahead. Only for a couple of seconds, but you'd been talking right along—"

"Did you see the Gold Man?" blurted Jazz and Ella gave him a sharp elbow in the ribs.

Ella's dad stood straight up in surprise. "Gold man?" he asked, and he looked bewildered.

"Oh, it was nothing," said Ella. "We'd been talking about a movie, and a Gold Man was—er—"

"I see," said her Dad. "You both saw the same film."

"Yes," said the two teenagers.

"Well, here's what's happening," said Ella's dad. "All of us— I mean, both families—we're going to stay at the Contemporary. So Jazz, your Mom and I decided to ask for rooms next to each other, and then we could do things together this week. Would you like that?"

Both Jazz and Ella grinned at the same moment, and agreed

with an enthusiasm that surprised Ella's dad. "Well, good," he chuckled. "I'm glad you two are getting along so well."

Jazz and Ella couldn't stop chatting with one another about the Gold Man and what he said to them until the plane started the process of landing. Jazz clutched at the armrests until his fingers turned white. Ella noticed how nervous he was and elbowed him. "Don't be so worried," she said. "This won't hurt at all."

"I know that is true", said Jazz. I just always hate this part of plane rides.

Indeed, Jazz felt a little bump and heard a noise like a 'thunk', and raised his head to look out the window. The plane rolled smoothly along the ground. His face turned pink, and he felt a little embarrassed. Ella turned to him. "See?" she said. "That's all there is to it."

"Yeah," he said, not looking up.

"Jazz," she said, "You know the worst part of any scary situation is how you feel before you do it. Once you're in it, it's never as bad as you thought it was going to be."

Jazz nodded. "We're okay, aren't we?" she persisted.

"Yes," he admitted.

Mr. Butler, Ella's dad, handed Jazz his sports bag from the overhead and Jazz carried it down the aisle toward the exit. The group climbed off the plane.

The two families decided to rent a large mini-van together and save some money. It was spacious enough for all the luggage, and all four people. Ella's dad offered to drive.

Jazz felt too excited to do much other than watch the road go by on Buena Vista drive. This was working out better than he could have hoped. Not only was he not going to be lonely but it looked as if he was going to have a cool adventure with his new friend who was turning out to be really fun to be with. After several minutes of driving, Ella nudged him and pointed. He spotted the Mouse Ears on top of the water tower and he realized again that this vacation was actually happening.

Jazz said, "I've always wanted to come back here. I was pretty little the last time we came."

"Me, too", said Ella.

Jazz's Mom turned around from the front seat and looked at them. "What do you guys want to do first?"

"Epcot," they said in unison, remembering the words of the Gold Man.

"Okay," said the two adults in the front, also in unison.

"Can you wait until tomorrow?" asked Jazz' s Mom.

The teens were a bit disappointed, but Ella's Dad said, "We kind of have to; our tickets start in the morning."

"Don't worry," said Mom. "We'll see everything."

She turned back to look out the front window and the two friends stared at one another. "What is happening with our parents?" asked Jazz, in a tiny whisper.

"I don't know," said Ella. "I haven't seen Dad this happy in so long. He doesn't stop smiling."

"He doesn't have to," shrugged Jazz.

Getting checked in at the Contemporary Hotel seemed to take forever. While the parents worked at registering, the teenagers explored. Jazz looked up and pointed at something that resembled a very modern white train.

"There's be the monorail. I read that they run on magnetism."

"It's too bad we can't use them to get to the Animal

Kingdom," said Ella.

Jazz considered. "Yea, I know", he said. "I think you drive or maybe take a bus."

Ella nodded and they continued their walk through the big lobby, looking back once in a while to keep an eye on their parents. The huge lobby seemed full of people, everyone bustling, hurrying from one place to another. They spent some time watching the people exit from the monorail, load up again, and then take off.

Ella and Jazz had a good laugh over the outfits a whole group of people were wearing. They were all dressed in neon orange shirts, which said "Meyer Family Reunion". "I bet more of their people are coming," whispered Ella. "Maybe we'll see them walking around the parks this week. Don't you think it would be fun to have a large family and have all of them meet here every year to be together for a whole week at Disney?"

"I bet they are all going to be staying here. That would be neat, but my family is really small. I wish I had a bigger family," Jazz said. "I don't have any cousins, or brothers, or anything."

"I know," said Ella. "I'm pretty much the same way. It would be fun, though."

At that moment she tugged at his arm and they saw her Father waving to them. They ran over to him. "Hey, you two, we have to decide on colors for our wristbands. We'll wear them all week to enter all the attractions and rides, get food, use the transportation system, and get into our rooms. What color do you want?"

Ella didn't hesitate. "Purple", she replied.

"Grey", said Jazz.

Later, they met their parents in front of an escalator that

seemed to go all the way to the ceiling. "Come on," said Jazz's Mom. "We're going up into the tower. We'll drop off our luggage at our rooms and then we'll do some exploring on the Monorail."

Two hours later, the two families returned to their rooms, which were right next to each other. Jazz's mom and he went into one room, while Ella and her dad went next door. Jazz and his mom unpacked, then he went outside and stood behind a guardrail, watching the trains come in.

Ella came out a few moments later, wearing a swim suit. "Can you swim?" she asked him.

"Sure," he said. "I was on the swim team at the YMCA last winter."

"Then put on your swim suit," she said. "You and I are going down to the pool."

The two of them goofed around in the beautiful pool for a while. Ella seemed to be as good a swimmer as Jazz, and they laughed, trying to dunk one another, until the sun started to go down.

Their parents arrived and walked over to the pool. Ella's dad had on shorts and a sport shirt, while Jazz's mom wore a skirt and a casual blouse. "Come on, you two," said his mom. "You have to go up and get changed for dinner."

They hustled back to their rooms, quickly showered and changed into clothes for dinner. Then they met in the hallway and hurried into an elevator. A man stood in the elevator and asked, "What floor?"

"We're going down to the pool area," said Ella.

The man smiled and pushed the button marked "1" and the elevator doors shut.

Jazz stood talking to Ella when suddenly it occurred to him that the man in the elevator looked very familiar. He also didn't think they had elevator operators at the hotel. He thought for a second about how to be polite and asked, "Excuse me, sir..."

But the elevator stopped and the entire car was flooded with golden light. The man turned to them and gave them a big, welcoming smile. "We meet again," he said. "Hello Jazz, hello Ella," said the Golden Man. "I'm sorry to stop you here and startle you."

"Well, we are rather surprised to see you here. We thought we wouldn't see you until the ride", said Ella.

"I understand," said the man. "Be at peace. You have nothing to be afraid of with me." The teenagers nodded, sensing that this man truly meant them no harm whatever.

"Yes," he said. "We are on the same side."

"We are?" said Jazz.

"Oh yes, definitely," he said. "On this side, we love good and truth."

Jazz and Ella both responded, "Yes", at the same time.

"I am sorry to appear like this," said the man. "But I cannot come to you when your parents can see me."

"Why?" asked Ella.

"Because they would not want you to do what we need you to do," said the Man. "We need you to make an important discovery."

"You do?" they asked in unison.

"Yes," said the Man. "Do you still have the Amulets? Are you protecting them?"

They nodded. "Here they are," said Jazz, holding his up as Ella produced hers.

"Good," said the Man. "Go to Spaceship Earth at Epcot and watch for Thucydides."

"For who?" questioned Ella and Jazz, but then the light vanished as quickly as it had appeared, and the elevator began to move again. They staggered a little, looked at one another quizzically, and shrugged their shoulders.

"Do you think we should tell someone about this?" said Jazz.

"I want to tell Dad," agreed Ella. "But no one except you and me seems to know what's happening. They don't see the light or the man."

"I know," he shrugged. "But this is kind of weird, isn't it?"

"I guess we just go along and see what happens," said Ella. "Do you feel like the man is—I don't know—evil?"

"No, not at all," said Jazz. "I feel wonderful when he's here. Like a warmth, and a quiet, like no one could hurt us at all, ever, when he's with us."

The door opened and Ella released his hand. "I guess there's no sense in being worried, right?"

"No, I don't think so," he said. "Let's try to have fun."

The families ate together at a sandwich area, their parents sitting opposite one another, and continued to talk, laugh, seeming to be having a great time together.

Jazz turned to his new friend. "They really like each other, don't they?"

"Ya, they really do", said Ella. "My dad hasn't looked at anyone like he looks at your mom for a good long time. Since Mom died."

"I know what you mean," said Jazz. "And my mom seems to be—softer?" Ella lifted an eyebrow and gave a little smile.

"I think I know what you mean," said Ella.

CHAPTER 3

That evening as Jazz was getting into bed, his mom came and sat down next to him. "You like Mr. Butler and Ella, I can see."

"Yes, I do, Mom," Jazz said. She rubbed his back.

"Do you mind if I went down to the restaurant area with Mr. Butler for awhile?" Mom asked.

Jazz hesitated. "Sure," he said. "I'll be all right."

"Look," said Mom. "Here's your cell phone. You know how to speed dial me, right?" Jazz nodded. "If you need anything, call me and I can be here in a couple minutes, okay?"

Jazz felt a little embarrassed. Of course he'd be okay. He wasn't a little kid anymore. Why would she think he would be upset with her going out for a bit? He'd stayed by himself many times before, and knew that Mom would be back a little later. "Sure, Mom."

"Okay, then," she said. She kissed his cheek and gave him a hug. "What do you want to do tomorrow?"

"I want to go to Epcot," he said. "I think Ella and her Dad want to go there too."

"Yes, they do," said Mom, grinning. "I just wanted to make sure that was okay with you. Okay to go right after breakfast?"

"Sure, that's great".

Jazz climbed under the covers and put on his earphones to

listen to his music as Mom left and shut the door. A moment later, he heard a tap, very light, on the door connecting the two rooms. He hopped out of bed, walked to the door and opened it.

Ella stood there, beaming at him. She had on a long white nightgown and she looked very pretty.

"Can we talk for a couple minutes?" she said, with her big smile on her face.

"Sure," he said. "What's up?"

She came into the room and sat down on the bed. He sat down next to her.

"Is something wrong?" asked Jazz.

"Kind of," she said. "I'm kind of nervous about what happened to us today."

"Yeah," he said. "I know. This kind of thing just doesn't happen to people. It's what you might expect to see if you go to a movie or read about it in a book, but never in real life."

"Exactly! Why us?" she asked, slapping the bed. "Are we imagining this? Are we just wanting something exciting to happen and so we see what we are hoping for or expecting? Why would they pick us?"

"No, we definitely are not imagining this, but I don't know why we have been chosen to do whatever they are wanting us to do," he admitted. "I mean I'm just a regular normal person. I live with my Mom in a normal house. We're not rich, and I'm not real smart or strong either. I have never been on any adventure that would make me qualified for some special task"

"No," said Ella. "No, me either! I mean, I get good grades, yeah, but I don't think I'm the smartest girl in our school. I play some sports and I can swim, but I feel like you. I'm just kind of ordinary."

"But we are definitely going to be asked to do something," said Jazz. "I don't know what. I guess we'll do it, huh?"

She thought for a moment. "I need to ask you something," she said. "Do you have the feeling that if we said 'no' that we wouldn't have to do it?"

He considered. "Yes, I do think that."

She was silent again. "What would you think if we said 'no'?

Jazz spoke up after a few moments. "I think this may be a chance for you and me to be something other than ordinary, like we are. I think maybe we could live our lives and never have to think about this again, if that's what we want to do."

She considered his words. "Sure, I agree with you," she said. "We could say 'no' to the Angel."

He was surprised. "An Angel?" he said. "I hadn't thought of that. Do you think that's what we saw?"

"I think it's most likely," she said. "I certainly don't think it's an outer space monster."

"No, I have to agree with you on that point", he laughed. "I felt like this man—well, he loved us. I know that sounds odd, but I am convinced he is giving us an opportunity to do something special."

"And if we do it, we'll be better than we ever would be otherwise."

Again he thought. "Yeah."

"I'm still kind of scared," she admitted.

"I guess I am a little scared,too. Especially since it's all so mysterious. We haven't been given any information at all about what we have to do," he said.

"My dad told me a story a while ago," she said. "Would you like to hear it?"

"Sure," he said.

"He told me that he tried out for football when he was in high school," she said. "He wanted to play Quarterback on the team. At practice one night, when they were just starting the season, the coach asked for a volunteer to play quarterback."

She paused. "Did your dad volunteer?" Jazz asked.

"No," she said. "No, he didn't. The coach picked someone else when no one volunteered."

"How did your dad feel?"

"He told me he felt dumb. But it did make him determined."

"Determined about what?"

"He told me that for the whole rest of his life up till now, he's never failed to try something because he felt afraid."

Jazz considered this. "How do you think he'd have done if he'd volunteered to play quarterback?"

"There's no way to tell, of course." she shrugged. "But he'll never know because he didn't try."

Jazz nodded. It was quite a lesson. "My mom had something like that happen to her," he said. "Not quite the same, but similar. When she was a little girl, she and her parents were visiting her mom's parents."

"Her grandparents," she said.

"Yeah, sure," he nodded. "Well, one night they asked her what she wanted to do. She spoke right up. 'I want to be a doctor,' she said.

"Wow," said Ella. "She's always wanted to be a doctor?"

"Yeah," said Jazz. "That's what she says. Anyway, her grandpa said, 'Don't be silly. You're not smart enough to be a doctor.'"

Ella sat with her mouth open, staring at him for a few

moments. "That wasn't very nice," she said, looking angry.

"No, I suppose not," agreed Jazz. "But she did go to Medical School, she did very well, and now she's – well, I think, anyway—she's a great doctor. People love her and respect her."

"I can see why," said Ella. "She's so nice. I really like her."

"I'm glad." said Jazz. "I think she's pretty cool for a mom."

The two teens sat in silence. "So we need to have courage too," said Ella. "Like our parents."

"Yeah," said Jazz. "We can't be afraid. I mean, we can be, but we can't back down from doing this just because we're not sure of what we are facing."

"Right," said Ella. "I know what you mean and I totally agree."

They sat and talked for a few more minutes, but finally Jazz said, "Ella, I'm really sleepy."

"I know," she said. "Can I sleep in here? I don't like being alone."

"Sure," he said, slipping under the puffy comforter on his bed. She climbed into the other large bed used by Jazz's mom. Both were asleep within minutes.

Their parents found them sound asleep some time later. They laughed when they saw them. Mr. Butler gently ruffled Ella's hair and guided her, still mostly sleeping, back to their room and into her own bed.

The next morning both families were up at 6:00 thanks to the wake-up calls that had been arranged the day before. They were all excited to start their vacation at Epcot. When Ella got up, she jumped into the shower and got dressed in record time. In the other room, Jazz also dressed quickly and the they met outside their rooms and went down to the breakfast buffet together.

Their parents joined them in about fifteen minutes and they all ate a huge breakfast at the buffet as they made plans for the day.

The two families drove together to EPCOT, parked, and then joined a large crowd waiting to get into the park for the early opening hours. The gates opened promptly at 8:00 a. m. and as soon as they passed through the turnstiles they headed straight to the pavilion called Fastrac. The families decided during breakfast to start there since it was supposed to be one of the rides where long lines would quickly form. They all had a great time designing their individual cars using a computer to pick out specific colors, wheels, engines and all the other design elements. Finally, they climbed into the cars and saw how their car compared to others during the exciting ride. From there, they went to Journey into Imagination, the Land, and The Living Seas, where they watched scenes from the Nemo movie and walked around the museum-like area after the ride.

"Mom," said Jazz. "Can we please go on Spaceship Earth?"

They all agreed and the group returned to the large silver sphere that dominated the entrance to Epcot. When they arrived, they found long lines. However, they saw it did keep moving, and so they got in the queue.

Ella and Jazz climbed into a car and sat together behind their parents. They noticed that their parents sat very close together, holding one another's hands.

The Time Vehicles moved slowly up into the massive ball called Spaceship earth, moving past the animatronic figures representing the Caveman era, ancient Egypt, and on up to the Golden Age of Greece. A figure stood there, talking in Greek as if lecturing a class of four students.

And the Golden Light returned.

The figure in the tableau turned to the ride, which had now stopped. Jazz and Ella looked at one another, and then back at the man. "Hello, dear ones," said the man. "Come up here." Looking around, they became aware that everything around them had been frozen in time.

The bar that secured them in their seats dropped back, and Jazz and Ella stood up and walked onto the platform. It never occurred to them that they should not exit the ride before it ended.

"How do you do," said the figure, speaking as if he did this to all the visitors to Spaceship Earth. "My name is Thucydides," he continued, "and these are my students."

"Please, sir," said Ella. "How is this possible?"

"It isn't," said the figure of Thucydides. "It can't happen. But we need for you to do something that is also impossible. That is why we have come to call you."

The four students sitting opposite the teacher murmured in agreement. Jazz and Ella looked around at them. They were, as the teens knew, only animatronic figures with fake skin, artificial bones and steel arms and legs. Yet at that moment they were alive, somehow. They were breathing, smiling, moving—everything that real people did.

"Who are you?" asked Ella. "You stand and sit here as moving statues, but you aren't now. Now you seem to be alive."

The teacher nodded. "Yes," he said. "We've been granted some magic here so that we can talk to you. But now you must return to your vehicle. Remember: learning is vital. Do your best to learn all you can. We are lifeless, but you are not. When people cease to learn, they cease to live."

The teens said goodbye and walked back to the Spaceship

Earth car and sat back down. "Ready?" asked Jazz.

"I think so," shrugged Ella. "This doesn't make any more sense than it did before the ride started."

"I agree, it's all very confusing," Jazz said. The restraining bar slid back down and real life returned as smoothly as it had paused. The figures in the Greek display were once again animatronic figures, not living and breathing as they had been a few moments before.

Jazz and Ella didn't say much as the ride ended a few minutes later. Their parents draped their arms around them as they stepped out of the carts onto the moving track and made their way out of the ride.

Jazz spoke to Ella as they came out into the brilliant Florida sunshine. "I think maybe we should tell them about what's going on."

She thought. "No, I don't agree," she said after a few moments. "First of all, they wouldn't believe it. No one would."

He shrugged. "Yeah, I guess that's true, isn't it."

She nodded. "Second of all, they'd want to protect us, and keep us from harm, and they'd try to help. I don't think they can. I think it's something we have to do on our own without them."

"Yeah," he said, but he didn't sound convinced, even to himself. Ella punched his arm.

"Look," she said. "Have you felt scared at any of the things that have happened to us?"

"No," he said. "No, I think I just don't like not knowing what's going to happen."

"I know," she said. "But Dad's always told me that no one is *ever* told what's going to happen before it does."

"Yeah, Mom says that to me, also."

"Right."

"So it's up to us to be brave and face it."

"Not only that," she said. "We haven't done anything wrong. We're not facing being punished for anything, right?"

"You're right," he said. "I guess we're being asked to do something for someone who can't do it. You remember they said we have to do it because we're kids."

"What're you two talking about?" asked Dad.

"Oh," said Jazz. "Just the ride. We want to go on Space Mountain tomorrow, okay?"

Their two parents looked at one another and smiled. His mom said, "Sure, we wanted to go to the Magic Kingdom anyhow. We'd better get there early, huh?" Everyone nodded in agreement. The crowds weren't bad in January, but getting into the parks early still seemed to be a good idea.

The group ate dinner that night in an Epcot Center restaurant in the Morocco Pavilion at The World Showcase. "I don't think I've ever had lamb," remarked Ella.

"It's yummy with this mint jelly," said Jazz's mom, handing it over.

"Do you think we'd better go back to the room after dinner?" asked Mr. Butler, looking amused.

Jazz's mom chuckled. "Well, since it looks like our two younger group members are going to fall asleep in the couscous, it might be a good idea. I think the only thing keeping them awake is the show put on by the belly dancers." The two teenagers looked exhausted, but they felt better after a great dinner.

CHAPTER 4

Jazz and Ella fell asleep almost as soon as they climbed into their beds in the tower at the Contemporary. Jazz and his mom had a much bigger room with two queen beds and a pullout bed.

Despite their exhaustion, their dreams were fiery. They didn't think they were in dreadful danger—at least they hoped that was the case—but they didn't know what they were facing and were nervous. Jazz woke up at 2:15 a.m. His mom had plugged in a night light in the washroom, and he looked deeply into the mirror as he washed his hands and face. *What are we going to do?* He wondered for perhaps the 950th time. He ran over everything he could remember the angel saying. He couldn't remember anything even resembling a clue.

He came out of the washroom and climbed back into bed.

"Jazz?" came the small whisper from the other side of the door, accompanied by a soft knocking.

"Yeah," he answered, opening the door to see his new friend standing there.

"Are you okay", asked Ella.

"Sure," he said, trying to make it sound like he was confident, smiling, and unafraid.

"Are you worried?"

"Of course not," he scoffed.

"Right," said Ella, coming over to sit next to him. "You know what?"

"What's that?" he asked.

"I'm not scared either," she said.

"You're as big a liar as I am," he smiled at her in the dim glow of the nightlight in the bathroom.

She gave a little snort that sounded like 'snirk' and put her hand over her mouth to keep from laughing out loud.

"We're alone, Jazz," she said. Jazz sat up and looked at his mom's bed. The covers were rumpled, like she'd slept in it, but she wasn't there now.

"Huh," he said. "Do you think that she went for a drink or something?"

"Possibly," she said. "I didn't think I'd fallen asleep, but I guess I must have. My dad is gone, too."

"Yeah," nodded Jazz. "Me neither. Where do you think she went?"

She made a quiet sound that sounded like a little cough. "Can't you guess?"

"No, I..." he began, but then didn't finish the sentence. "Oh," he said. He realized that Mom had gone out with Ella's dad.

"Do you think you can get back to sleep, Jazz?"

He checked how he felt. "Yeah, I think so."

"Are you worried about your Mom?"

"No, I'm not," he said. "No. Not at all. She knows what she's doing. Besides, I can see how much she likes you and your Dad."

"Let's go back to sleep," she said. "I'm pretty sure every-thing's okay."

She stood and started to go back to her room. But she suddenly doubled back, sat next to him and wrapped her arms around her friend. Then she stood.

"Don't you listen to those idiots at your school, Jazz," she said. "Don't you listen. You're a really neat kid. I'm glad I met you."

He mumbled thanks. Then he realized he needed to say something, too. "I think you're great, Ella. I'm sure glad we met here."

Then she was back in her bed.

Jazz snuggled down into his warm, comfortable bed at the Contemporary Hotel. He lay on his side, aware that he felt better than he had felt since he was little. He felt confident. He was about to doze away when he heard a little click and the door to the room opened. He cracked an eye and saw his mother looking into the room.

"He's fine," Mother said in a whisper. "Sound asleep. I'm kind of tired myself. Thanks for the company. I'll see you in the morning for another magical day", she laughed.

"Good," said Ella's dad. "Sleep well."

The door shut. Jazz's mom went into the bathroom to get ready for bed so as not to wake Jazz.

CHAPTER 5

In the early morning, Mom shook Jazz awake. He came awake with a start, having been jolted out of a nightmare with golden people turning into large talking creatures. He saw his Mom and started to speak, but she put a finger against her lips. "Come on. I think the others are still asleep," she said. "Get your clothes on and meet me in the hall."

Jazz jumped into a quick shower and dried off, and then slipped into some clothes. He let himself out of the room, wondering why they were leaving without Mr. Butler and Ella, and met his mom in the hallway.

"I thought it might be nice to have a nice breakfast together, just the two of us", Mom said.

"Sure", said Jazz.

They took the elevator to the Monorail Level and found a train to take them to the Magic Kingdom. Mom, however, had them disembark at The Polynesian Resort, and they made their way to a restaurant. Jazz ordered a big breakfast, but Mom asked for fresh pineapple and coffee.

They chatted while they waited for their food, his mom asking him how he was enjoying the trip, was he having a good time with Ella, did he like the room and the restaurants, and so on.

"Ella and her father will meet us here in about 45 minutes,"

Mom told him. "As you asked, we're going to the Magic Kingdom today. How does that sound?"

Jazz hadn't said much, he realized, and nodded his head before speaking. "Yeah, Mom. Everything has been wonderful."

"You really seem to be enjoying Ella, too," said Mom.

Jazz nodded.

Mom cleared her throat and looked like she was about to speak again, but the waiter showed up and set their breakfasts in from of them.

Mom and the waiter chatted, and a busboy poured Mom some more coffee. Then they were alone, and Mom asked a little grace.

"What's going on, Mom?" asked Jazz. He was starting to become concerned.

Mom nodded. "I'm fine, Jazzy," she said. "I need to ask you a big question, and I don't know how to do it." She hadn't called him "Jazzy" for a very long time.

Jazz poured some syrup over his French toast and began to eat while he waited. At last Mom spoke.

"Jazz, I've been alone for several years, you know," she said. "I've really missed having a person to share life with me."

Now Jazz understood. "You want to get married," he said.

Mom hesitated for just a moment. Then she mumbled, "Yes, Jazzy, I do."

"Mr. Butler?" he asked.

"Yes, Honey," said Mom.

Jazz put his fork down and picked up his napkin. To his embarrassment, he started to get teary-eyed.

"Does that mean you don't want me to marry him?" asked Mom, when a few moments had elapsed.

"No," said Jazz. "He seems to be a very nice man."

"He is," said Mom. "I've been seeing him for some time, though you didn't know it. My medical office is in the same building as his. We met in the elevator and began meeting for lunch. Oh, he's an architect. Somewhat famous for the buildings and some homes he's designed. We ate lunch every day we could manage it for several months. Then we began having dinner. I'd never met Ella before this trip, just like you'd never met her or her father."

"Yeah," said Jazz.

"We have been talking about marriage and everything seems to be working out so well since we have all been together here at Disney that, well, we really would like to get married here," said Mom. That is, if you and Ella approve.

"Here?" asked Jazz. He found himself recovering from the initial shock.

"Yes, over at the Wedding Chapel at the Grand Floridian Resort," smiled Mom. "We want you and Ella to be part of it: you to be the best man for Mr. Butler and Ella to be my maid of honor. We've ordered tuxedos for you two men, and I have a dress I bought for Ella as a surprise."

Jazz hadn't seen his mom so excited in a very long time so he cautiously asked, "When?"

"We thought Friday, unless you have some objection," said Mom.

Jazz, feeling numb and unable to respond, managed a nod.

"We're also going to stay here for a few days longer," said Mom. "We'll go home Monday. Mr. Butler and I are going to Fort Lauderdale for a little honeymoon."

"What about me and Ella?" he asked.

"Well, we plan to sell Mr. Butler's condominium, and we're going to live, at least for a time, in our house," smiled Mom. "That way, you and Ella can continue in school without interruption."

"Mom?" he asked.

"Yes, Honey," she smiled.

"What about us?" he asked.

"You mean, you and me?" Mom asked.

He nodded, not wanting to disappoint her, but feeling a little conflicted. She took a second to compose an answer. "Jazz, nothing will ever change the fact that you are my son," she said. "No one will ever separate us, never. You'll always be precious to me."

Again Jazz nodded. "But the relationship of a man and a woman in marriage is far different than the mother and son relationship," Mom told him. "Mr. Butler and I will have a bond that goes beyond that. You'll have a family of your own in some years. You will give me grandchildren. But you'll always be my son, and nothing will ever change the relationship I have with you. Understand?"

Jazz wasn't completely sure he did understand, but he managed a nod. "You've gotten used to having me to yourself for some years now," said Mom. "And I've loved every minute. But there is no limit to the amount of love that one person can have. It can always expand to include others. I won't stop loving you because I get married. My love will expand to include Mr. Butler and Ella. It already has."

At that moment Mr. Butler spoke up from behind his mother. "You told him," he said, beaming ear to ear.

"Yeah, she did," said Jazz. He rose and shook Mr. Butler's

hand. He was struggling, but wanted to be gracious. Now Ella scurried up to him and embraced him.

Of all the things that had happened in the last few days, that hug meant more that anything. To know that Ella liked him, and could learn to love him as a brother, just might be the best part of this whole marriage.

The four of them sat together and chatted about the marriage and what would happen over the next several months, getting more enthusiastic the longer they talked. It wasn't long before Jazz began to realize this might be the best thing that could happen to him. Instead of just one person who cared about him and love him, he would now have a whole family just like everyone else.

At last Ella looked at Jazz and he nodded, knowing what she meant with that look. "Dad," said Ella. "Would you excuse us? We want to go into the Magic Kingdom."

"Do you want us to come with you?" asked Mom.

"How about if we meet you?" Said Jazz. "In an hour, at Big Thunder Railroad."

Their parents agreed and smiled as Jazz and Ella went out to the Monorail. They had to stand until the Monorail stopped in front of the Magic Kingdom so they couldn't really carry on a conversation. They exited the Monorail, ran to the park entrance, pressed their bracelets against the Mickey face at the gate, and walked into the park.

CHAPTER 6

As they headed up Main Street toward the Fairy Castle, Ella took his arm. "Are you okay?" she asked.

"Yeah," he said. "Fine. I'm just so surprised. I had no idea my mom was seeing anyone."

"I know," she said. "I had a feeling something special was going on between them even when we were in the plane, but I was totally surprised by the marriage thing. They must've had some reason not to tell us beforehand."

"Parents," muttered Jazz, and Ella laughed.

"So I guess we're going to be step-brother and step-sister, huh?"

"That's fine with me," said Jazz. "In fact, that's one of the best parts."

She smiled at him and they turned east toward the imposing Space Mountain Attraction. "Oh boy," said Ella. "I forgot to be nervous about what we're going to do."

"I know," he returned. "Now I'm nervous about it again."

"Okay," she said. "We won't be. It's nothing we can't handle."

"Right," said Jazz.

The line as always was long at Space Mountain, but at least it kept moving. Within a half hour, they were inside and moving to sit in the vehicle. Before they sat, she leaned up and kissed his cheek.

"We'll be okay, Jazz," she said.

"I know," he said. He took a seat behind her and the restraint bar snapped into place. The little car began to slide along.

Space Mountain Rollercoaster flies in the dark, and in moments their car began to climb upwards, clanking as it went.

The car reached the top and started down into the darkness. The speed increased as they went careening down the other side, and then zooming around corners so fast they couldn't catch their breath. Ella gave a little scream—

And then everything stopped.

CHAPTER 7

Jazz opened his eyes and looked around. He could see the inside of Space Mountain, and the lights were getting brighter.

"Are you okay?" asked Ella, turning to look back at him.

"Yeah," he said. "Sure, I'm fine. What happened?"

"All I know is the car stopped all of a sudden and the lights went on," she said. "We also seem to be all alone in here."

"I don't think we're really inside Space Mountain anymore," he said, looking around.

"And I'm pretty sure this isn't Kansas, either," she noted. Jazz seemed to notice that she didn't sound scared at all now.

"Like in *The Wizard of Oz*, huh?"

"Yeah," she giggled. "Come on. I don't think we're supposed to stay here. Let's go."

They pushed on the restraining bar, which plopped out of the way, and Jazz climbed out onto a walkway next to the car. "You think this is here to evacuate the ride?"

"Yeah," she shrugged, noticing the echo as they spoke. They climbed up to the top of the stairs and then back down to the loading platform. No one stood in line, no attendants stood by to help people into the cars for the ride, and no one called out, either. Space Mountain was empty except for Jazz and Ella.

They walked through the reception area and saw the

entrance. As they walked, they remained alert, but Ella spoke: "Do you think we're the only people here? I mean, anywhere?"

"It's possible," he said. "If what happened to us now is possible, I guess anything is."

They emerged into the Florida sunshine. Space Mountain seemed to be the only building anywhere. They saw grass, tall and waving, but no palm trees, no Magic Kingdom, nothing that they expected.

"What do we do?" asked Jazz. "I have no idea, do you?"

Ella thought, and they stared at the landscape. "Wait a second," said Jazz. He reached under his shirt and pulled out the Amulet.

"Of course," said Ella. She pulled out her amulet. The two friends held them up to the light and as they looked, the amulets transformed. They expanded to a great circumference and turned transparent. Through the enlarged circles, they saw yet another landscape. "Come on," said Ella, and they stepped into the circles.

Immediately the circles compressed again into the amulets and the friends stood in a dark, barren landscape, devoid of grass or trees or any sort of foliage. They stood on absolutely bare ground, rocky and cruel.

"Yick," said Ella. "What a miserable place."

"Yeah," he agreed. "Do you think we're supposed to be here?"

Ella held up her amulet, and they peered into the opening it created in the air. Through it, they could see the landscape they'd just left. "I don't know if we're supposed to be here," she said. "But it looks like we can get back when we want to."

"Okay," he said. "I guess we might as well explore."

They started to walk across the rock. Fortunately, Florida had been a little chilly that morning and they'd both dressed in jackets and blue jeans with their jogging shoes. Although they were used to cool weather, this air tended to chill them.

Ella gave a little shudder. "Not much fun here," she said.

"Like walking in jello," he noted. " The air feels—what? Thick? Can you think of a better word?"

She shook her head. "Chilling. Heavy. Unpleasant."

"Where do you think this is?"

"I haven't an idea," she said. "I know I've never been here."

In a moment, however, they saw what appeared to be two people walking slowly across the terrain toward them.

"Who's that?" asked Ella, squinting.

"I guess they'll tell us," said Jazz.

The people seemed to be plodding, reluctant to move, unhappy to be in this place. In moments, though, Ella and Jazz could see their features.

"My Gosh," said Ella. "That looks just like—"

"My father," said Jazz.

At the same moment Ella finished her sentence. "Mom!"

They turned to look at one another. At the same time, they said, "How did they get here?"

The woman raised a hand in greeting. "Hello, Ella."

She advanced toward Ella, with a big smile on her face. She extended her arms asking for an embrace.

"Jazz," said the man. "You've grown, Son." He also was smiling and he crossed toward Jazz with his hand outstretched toward him.

"Mom," said Ella.

"Dad," said Jazz.

Ella turned to him. "That's your father?" she gasped.

"Yeah," said Jazz. "And she's your Mom?"

"This isn't right," said Ella.

"Everything's fine, Honey," smiled Mrs. Butler. Ella drew back so as not to be touched by the woman. At the same time Jazz dodged away from the man.

"No," said Jazz. "You can't be here. You've never wanted anything to do with me. Why would you come here to see me?"

"Mom, you aren't here," said Ella, a tremor of fear in her voice. You died several years ago."

The two adults laughed.

"Is that what she told you?" said the man. "Jazz, listen. I've been doing everything in my power to get to see you—"

"Is that what he told you?" said the woman at the same time. "That's terrible, to tell a little girl such a horrible lie—"

"It isn't a lie," screamed Ella. "Go away! I don't want to hug you. I don't want to touch you!"

"You aren't my Father!" yelled Jazz at the same time.

Everything stopped. The man and woman stared at Jazz and Ella, and as they watched, the two figures began to—dissolve—in front of them. Their bodies turned pale and cracks appeared, and the two figures collapsed to the ground, turning to dust. A sharp wind blew and the dust swirled away.

"What happened?" asked Jazz, rubbing his eyes as if he'd just awakened from a horrid dream.

Ella turned to him, sobbing. Jazz, embarrassed, wrapped his arms around her and hugged. Then he began to cry also.

They stood there together for a long time, their bodies shaking with terror and dread at what they'd seen. Two people they'd loved but could not have possibly seen, had disintegrated before their eyes and it terrified them.

"O brother," said Jazz. "Who would do such a cruel thing?"

"Who could do such a thing?" asked Ella.

"I think this is a place where we have to face bad things that have happened to us," said Jazz.

Ella pulled a handkerchief from a pocket in her jeans. She wiped her eyes and blew her nose. "Well, that was really bad, I'll say that!"

Jazz also dried his tears by pressing his eyes against his tee-shirt sleeve.

"What do you think?" asked Jazz.

"I guess I've never let myself think about my Mom," she said. "I guess I felt that if I ignored being sad, eventually the feeling would go away."

Jazz considered. "Yeah, me too," he agreed. "I know Mom told me that they didn't get divorced because of me, but I didn't believe it, you know?"

"Why did you think that?" she asked.

"Because—because I came between them," he stammered. "They couldn't have the marriage they should have had because of me."

"I know that isn't true," said Ella.

"How do you know that?" asked Jazz. "You don't know—"

"I've met your Mom," said Ella. "I know she loves you. Anyone can see that. She's a person with a great deal of love to give, Jazz."

They stood in silence. At last Ella said, "Maybe you're right. Maybe we have come to a place where we have to face our fears".

"I think so," said Jazz. They started across the barren

landscape again. After about a hundred yards they saw a door, like a classroom door. They walked up to the door and peered inside.

"Do you recognize it?"

"Yes," said Jazz. "It's the door to the library at our junior high."

"Is this where something bad happened to you"? she asked.

"Yes", he whispered. Hesitating, he added, "some boys were really mean to me here".

"Right," said Ella. "I think this is for you, Jazz".

"Why do you say that?" he stalled. But, in his heart, he knew she was right.

"I think you have to face the boys who tormented you in this room," she said. "You didn't defend yourself against them and it is still haunting you, isn't it? Deep down you are still afraid of them."

"Yes," he whispered.

"Come on," she said. "I'll go with you."

He walked forward. When they got to the door, though, she found that she couldn't pass through the open door. Jazz stepped inside without trouble. "This is just for you, Jazz," she said. "I'm sorry, but I guess I'm not allowed to go with you."

He nodded. Now he knew what to do.

He turned left. Mrs. Hurley, the librarian, was talking about something called the Dewey Decimal System, but he'd heard this and learned it once before. He walked to the table.

There they sat—the three eighth graders who had terrified and bullied him. Albert Thomas was a bit smaller than Jazz, with greasy blond hair and a sneering expression. Bill Kidd, short and arrogant, looked up as Jazz approached and laughed that insolent, laughing snort of his. Frank Gale, the weasely hanger on of the group was last, bigger than Jazz, dumber than a lump of granite, profane and loud.

"Well, here he is, boys," said Albert. "Jazzy the dork." He launched a profane guffaw at Jazz.

"Hey Weesey," said Bill. Frank said something else.

"Okay, I guess I have to face you," said Jazz. "I have to confront you. If you want to fight with me, come on. I'll fight all three of you. Now."

Jazz fought to hold back the tears, but not out of fear. Just pure anger and resentment at these three thugs who'd teased him for a year, both here and in the hallways of the school. "I'm not giving you power over me any more."

The three bullies attacked him all at the same time. They hit him, punched him and kicked him, but Jazz screamed and fought back, swinging and kicking fiercely. Albert backed away, holding his bleeding nose. Bill bent over, crying, clutching his stomach. Frank turned and ran---

And then it was over. The three evaporated and the library melted away. He once again stood in the gray, rocky landscape they'd come to. He didn't feel any pain, or soreness at all.

Ella, no longer excluded from the memory, came over to him. "Did they hurt you?" she asked.

"Yeah, they hurt," he said. "But they won't any more. I stood up to them. That part of my history is resolved, I think."

"Okay," she said. "You were very brave, Jazz."

"I'm learning something important here," he said. "I have to go straight at what scares me. Don't back away. If people attack me, or bad things happen, I don't just have to live with it or put up with it."

"You don't have to back away from bullies, either," added Ella. "Make them accountable for what they do. Let them feel the shame of tormenting another person the rest of their lives."

"Shame?" he said.

"Yeah," she said. "They get to remember that they hurt someone else, physically and emotionally. That they damaged someone. That ought to be a memory for the rest of their lives that will continue to haunt them forever."

They continued to walk toward some sort of a light that they saw in the east. "Always go right at bullies," she said.

"Yeah," he said. "Sure, they can hurt you with physical attacks, but they can't hurt you as much as..."

Abruptly, they stood in a gymnasium. They recognized it in the same moment.

"Why are we in the gym at Harrison?" asked Jazz. "Nothing ever happened to me here. I..." He broke off. "Oh," he said. "This is for you, isn't it."

"Yes," she whispered. "I recognize it now. It's Cheerleading tryouts. Last fall."

"I didn't know you were a cheerleader," he said, eyebrows raised. "Did I forget?"

"No," she said. "I didn't make it."

"You?" he said, amazed. "But you're so..."

He broke off. His friend looked miserable. She had tears in her eyes.

"What happened?" he asked, but Ella walked forward toward a tall girl who looked just like her. And he realized that was her. Ella stopped, turned and took one step back —

And merged into herself.

"All right," yelled Mrs. Turpin, the girls' PE teacher and

cheerleading sponsor. "Here we go. Ella, you're first."

Ella stood and put on a big smile. As Jazz watched, she did three flips, a cartwheel, and wound up in the splits.

There wasn't a sound from the girls who were watching the tryouts. They looked angry and sullen, with surly expressions on their faces.

"That sucked!" One of the girls screamed.

"Boo!" yelled several other girls. Ella took a seat, red-faced and hurt. Mrs. Turpin, angry at their rude outbursts, spoke sharply to the girls.

The noise stopped, but the girls turned away from Ella as she sat on the bleachers. Several other girls did the same routine, but to Jazz's uncertain eyes, none of them were as good as Ella. Her routine had, as far as he could see, been flawless. The others were nowhere near as expert as she.

He sat on the bleachers as Ella came over to join him. They watched for a few more minutes, and then Mrs. Turpin walked over to the large group of girls who had been so nasty. She talked with them for a few moments. Then she came to where Ella sat with Jazz.

"Ella," she said. "I'm so sorry. You did a beautiful job. But the other girls all scored you the lowest."

"What!" yelled Jazz. Mrs. Turpin didn't react. Jazz realized she couldn't hear him. She continued to speak to Ella.

"They won't cheer with you," she said. "They told me that if you make the squad they'll all quit. I don't know what to do. I have to have a cheerleading squad."

"That's all right, Mrs. Turpin," said Ella, sitting next to Jazz. "I guess I understand."

The gym began to fade, and Ella and Jazz found themselves

in the bleak landscape of rock and cold again. Ella was still crying.

"They did that—threatened Mrs. Turpin—because they don't like you?"

Ella nodded. "I've never been popular," she said. "Never in with the popular group. I like things they don't like, and I won't drink, or go out just to make out with boys, all that."

"You're my best friend," he said. "Do I count?"

"Of course you do," said Ella. "You're my best friend, too. When I saw you on the plane by yourself I knew we'd be good friends. I think we always will be," she added.

He took her hand and squeezed. She pulled her hand away and hugged him again. "You're so sweet to me," she said. "You aren't like the other kids at the school. Don't try to be like them. Just be yourself, okay?"

"Sure," he said. They sat like that for a few moments. "Wait a minute," said Jazz.

She drew back and peered at him. "Why did we have to see that?" he asked.

"I don't know," she said. Then she added, "No, I think I do know. We had to see that because—"

"Because that's where we always are," he said. "We have allowed those events and others like it dominate who we are."

"Yes," she said. "We have to let those horrible things go. They aren't supposed to make us miserable. Instead we're supposed to learn from them and not let them destroy us."

"Okay—" he said.

"No, Jazz, not okay," she said. "I mean it. We have to promise to re-program our minds."

"Can you do it?" he asked.

"Dad told me that he read somewhere that the brain can be re-wired," she said. "We can choose what we want to think or dwell upon. Or maybe choose not to let certain things take over our thoughts if we don't want them to."

"I think you're right," he agreed. "I don't have to be that boy that kept getting beaten up and having his feelings hurt because that's over, in the past."

"Yes," she said. "And those girls who were so mean to me don't get to hurt me any more. I promise. I'll never have to see them or associate with them again."

"But the teacher…"

"She wasn't a real teacher," said Ella. "No real teacher would let me be bullied like that. She never stepped in and told the girls off and never protected me."

They looked down. They realized that they were walking on grass. Now they felt sunshine on their face. The sky had turned blue, a few fluffy clouds just in sight. "What happened?" asked Jazz.

"I don't know," she said. "I think we need to go back to Space Mountain, though. Let's finish the ride. We still have the amulets, and they still seem to work, and…"

She broke off. "Yeah," said Jazz. "Let's go."

Ella held up her amulet at the same time he did and they took one step forward. In the next instant, they found themselves back in the Space Mountain ride, secured in their seats and the carts rocketing around. They zoomed up and down, laughing and gasping, as the pitch-dark room resounded with the screams of other riders.

CHAPTER 8

When they pulled in, the attendants helped them out of the ride. Ella was red cheeked and exhil-arated from it, though Jazz felt like cold gravy.

"Yuck," he said. "I don't do well on roller coasters."

She took his arm. "C'mon," she giggled. "You'll feel better when we walk around."

They walked back toward the Fairy Castle and met their parents waiting for them by the Pirates of the Caribbean ride. The children sat with their parents in the gentle ride, amused by the all of the animatronic figures they encountered.

"A lot of this was in the movie *Pirates of the Caribbean*,'" said Jazz. "The one with Johnny Depp, I remember."

Ella commented on the humorous antics of all the figures they passed as they glided through the ride. "Yeah," she said. "I thought it was a fun movie." Jazz agreed and told her that *Pirates of the Caribbean* was one of his favorite movies.

The group ate lunch at the restaurant, Be Our Guest, and were able to snag a table in the ballroom section which looked like it came straight out of the movie: Very fun and the food was not only plentiful, but delicious. After forcing down dessert, they all spent the afternoon enjoying the rest of the Magic Kingdom. At last they made their way to the Monorail and returned to the hotel for a couple of hours before dinner.

Jazz's mom put on her robe when they returned to the room and laid down on her bed. "I think I'll just close my eyes for a bit," she said. She fell asleep in moments.

Jazz heard a light tapping on the door between the rooms, opened it, and found Ella. She peeked into the room and saw Jazz' Mom asleep on the bed.

"Come on," she whispered, beckoning him to follow her. "My dad"s asleep, too. I left him a note that we'd be at the pool."

Jazz threw on his swim suit and the two of them hurried down to the pool. They swam, played in the pool and relaxed on a couple of deck chairs.

"That was a fun day," she said.

"Fun?" he said. "Reliving those awful things was fun?"

"I'm not going to focus on those things," she said. "I'm going to move on with my life and put those memories away. And you promised to do the same, remember?" The sun was starting to go down now, and they pulled a couple of the pool towels over themselves. An hour and a half later, their parents found them sound asleep under the towels. They had to shake them to wake them up.

"Dress up a bit," said Ella's dad. "We'll have dinner in Fulton's Crab House over in the Downtown Disney."

They both ran up to change and rejoined them at the pool, where their parents were enjoying a couple of drinks while they waited for Ella and Jazz to return. "Are you ready at last?" teased Jazz's mom, and they went out front to the car.

The seafood at the restaurant was amazing. Both Ella and Jazz had grown up in the Midwest and had never experienced fresh seafood, directly from the ocean to their plates. Only under extreme pressure from their parents did Jazz and Ella give up on the idea of having a specialty burger and fries. Jazz, with help from the waiter, ordered a piece of Ahi Tuna covered with a crabmeat spread, and Ella had the daily special, which was a very fresh Mahi-mahi. They both agreed they had made the right choice, loving every mouthful. After dinner they all decided to try the chocolate mousse for dessert. It was smooth as silk, very rich, and they were quite happy with their dessert decisions. After a walk through the Disney Market, they headed back to the Contemporary. Jazz and Ella went upstairs while their parents went down to the fourth floor lounge.

"What do we do?" asked Ella. "I was hoping we'd get another message, weren't you?" She sat on the edge of the sofa next to him.

"Yeah," he said. "What do we do now?"

"I have an idea," she said. "What time does the Magic Kingdom open tomorrow?"

"8:00," he said. "Why don't we try to be the first in line when it opens."

She thought. "Look," she said. "Let's get up about 6:30, and we'll go down and hustle over there. I think we need to go on Space Mountain again."

He considered. "Yeah. How do we get up that early?"

"I have a timer on my phone and can set it to vibrate so it doesn't my dad. You can do the same," she said.

"Great idea," he said.

"Okay," said Ella and went over to the connections door. "Let's turn in so we are ready to get going early."

He shut his eyes, and thought that for sure he'd never fall asleep. He settled in, and decided to make a good effort. It took him all of five minutes to fall into a deep sleep.

CHAPTER 9

Suddenly Jazz awoke to the vibration of his pillow. For a minute he was confused, but then he remembered their plan to get an early start. He knocked softly on the door between the rooms.

"I'll be right out," she whispered, and quickly grabbed her Mickey bracelet, stuffed some personal items into her purse, and left a note for her dad.

Jazz had taken a shower the night before and he was dressed and waiting in the hallway when Ella came out, wearing jeans, a nice tee-shirt, and a white jacket.

"I left a note for our parents," she said. "We'll be fine. We may even be back before they wake up. Here, I grabbed a couple of snacks to eat on the way."

"That was a great idea. Thanks", said Jazz

The Monorail stood waiting for them and they hurried into it. They rode around to the Magic Kingdom and ran toward Space Mountain.

The ride was just opening as they ran up the ramp. They hurried in to the exhibit and sat at the front of a car. Again, the ride clanked into motion and started up the first ramp. Down it hurtled, around a twisting curve and--

--stopped. A bright light shone all around them. The restraint fell back and Jazz and Ella clambered out.

Once again they found that The Magic Kingdom had vanished, and they ran into the grassy meadow where they had been yesterday. As they hurried, they saw a range of mountains in the distance.

"Mountains in Florida?" said Jazz, bewildered.

"Remember? We're not in Florida any more. We're somewhere else."

Jazz thought. "Yeah," he said. "But I don't know where this is. We've been shot through space somehow. We could be on the other side of the Galaxy."

"So someone—whoever is doing this to us—is capable of moving us supernatural distances?"

"Well, does this look like anything you've seen on earth?" asked Jazz.

She shrugged. "I guess not," she said. "I would just love to know who is doing all this."

"Me, too," he said, as they walked along. "But I don't feel like we're dealing with Evil today. Yesterday, yeah—those figures that seemed to be our parents were out to harm us."

"I believe you're right about that," she said. "They weren't our parents, though."

"No, of course not," Jazz agreed. "But they seemed to be. They appeared to us as if they were."

"But why?"

"So we'd see our parents as enemies?"

"Huh?" she said after thinking through this idea.

"Well, one thing that makes people strong is a strong family," he said. "Agreed?"

"I guess so," she said. "My Dad is a big strength for me. I mean, he always has loved me and supported me. When Mom died, he made a point of standing with me. He took me with him to meet our relatives in California, whom I'd never met."

"My mom was that way for me, too," he said. "She knew how badly it hurt not to have my dad around. I missed him like crazy. She threw baseballs and played catch with me, coached my Little League and Pony League baseball teams, got me into swimming — she did all she could to make up for the void left by my dad walking out on us. She even cut way back on her hours at the Clinic to be home at night with me."

"That's great," said Ella.

"I think whoever is doing this wants me to be alienated from my mom. And you from your dad. We really can't let that happen."

Ella agreed, and in a few more moments they had walked to the edge of a high cliff. "It looks like one of the areas along the Pacific Coast Highway," she said. "Dad drove me along U. S. 1 in California last year. It was so beautiful".

"I've never seen the Pacific Ocean," he admitted. "This vision must be for you."

"I think so," she said. She stood on the edge of a cliff, looking down on the four lane highway that was carved into the cliff. On the other side of the road, the cliff again fell away into the ocean.

"This is creepy, just standing here right on the edge," said Jazz.

Ella nodded. "I've always had nightmares about falling off a cliff," she said. "I always wake up before I land. My heart is beating, I sometimes scream — "

"So you're afraid of heights?" he said, trying to be a gentle as possible.

"Yeah, I guess so," she agreed. "So what do I do?"

"Maybe you have to confront your fear," he suggested.

"You mean, jump?" she screamed.

"I don't know," he said. "I do know we were both nervous about getting on Space Mountain yesterday. You had a blast, though. You were laughing and all that."

"That's true," said Ella, calming down a bit.

"I'm not really afraid of heights," he said. "But I can't see how jumping here would benefit us, can you?"

"As you said, it's for me," she said. "I have to go right at something that frightens me; not back away."

He took her hand. "Okay," he said. "Let's face it together."

She looked at him. "Right."

They jumped.

CHAPTER 10

They picked up speed as they went down. At first, the speed frightened them, and even got worse, but Jazz yelled, "I know this is what we were supposed to do."

Ella nodded. "If we do hit and die, we'll be together anyway, right?" They tumbled down, faster, and faster.

And then…

Their speed slowed very gradually, and the ground finally came up to meet them. When they touched down, they were as comfortable as if they were climbing out of bed in the morning.

Jazz and Ella remembered to bend their knees, as you're supposed to when you land, but the landing didn't hurt. The relief they felt came out in an explosion of laughter. "That wasn't so bad, was it?" said Jazz.

She smiled. "Wow! That was really fun! Do you think we can do it again?" Both of them laughed.

"I think you were just supposed to learn a lesson," he told Ella.

"I know," she said. "I know that's true. I'm trying to pull it together."

"It sure isn't that we ought to jump from a tremendous height," he commented.

"No," she agreed. "Let me try. I think this lesson was that facing and going right at something that frightens me is the thing to do. It's just another confirmation of what we have to learn through all these experiences."

"Yep," said Jazz, after thinking it over for a few moments. "I can see how that can be true for me, too."

"What do you mean?" she asked.

"Well, like on the airplane when we were coming here," he said. "I mean to Florida. You came and sat with me. You didn't seem to be afraid of me, or shy."

"You're kind of shy, aren't you," she said.

"Yeah," he said. "I know I would never have have come over and introduced myself to you."

She mulled at that for a second. "I've never been afraid to go up to people and say hi," she said, slowly. "But you say you are?"

"I always have been," he said. "I can remember hiding behind my mom when her patients would greet me in a store, or something, or when I'd meet people at church, y'know…"

She nodded. He went on. "And then you came over, and you were so friendly, and you're so pretty, and …" He broke off, embarrassed.

"You think I'm pretty?" she said.

"Of course I do," he said. "I think you're great. But you're also so friendly, and you laugh a lot…" He realized that he was red-faced with embarrassment again.

"Well, thank you," she said. She took his hand and they walked in silence down the four lane highway. Jazz looked west, or what seemed to be west—out over the ocean, anyhow.

"Why did you do that?" he asked. "Come over to talk to me, I mean? The airplane wasn't more than half full."

"Because I wanted someone to talk to, I guess," she said.

"Also, I sort of knew you from school—I mean, I recognized you. I think also that I realized that my dad wanted to talk to your mom, and they wanted to sit together. You seemed to be my best chance at having some company on the flight."

They talked a little more. They soon realized that no cars went by on the road. They seemed to be all alone, in fact, the only inhabitants of this strange world where you jumped off cliffs and didn't get hurt.

An eagle screamed overhead, and they looked. "It's an American Bald Eagle," said Jazz.

"Yeah," said Ella. "My dad has a friend, Mr. Toll, who lives on a lake in Northern Wisconsin. He pointed out an eagle's nest to me way up in a tree."

"That must have been cool to see," said Jazz.

"Even better than that," said Ella. "Dad and Mr. Toll took me out fishing. I caught a smallmouth bass, and I was about to throw it back when Mr. Toll said, 'Let's feed the eagles.'"

"You mean he fed the fish to the eagles?"

"Yeah," she continued. "He stood up in the boat and began waving it back and forth in the air. Sure enough, one of the eagles took off and came flying toward us. I could hear the beat of its wings and see it looking. Mr. Toll threw the fish way up into the air and the eagle caught it."

"Gosh," said Jazz. "How neat that must have been."

"The eagle wheeled around and headed back across the lake to its nest," said Ella. "We could hear little screams from the baby eagles in the nest and just could see their heads poking up as the eagle fed them the fish I'd caught."

They talked and kept walking. "Where are we going?" asked Ella.

"I don't have a clue," he said. "You had to face your fear. I reckon I'll have to face mine," he added, staring at his feet.

Ella didn't answer. He turned to her—

But she wasn't there. He looked around. "Ella?" he said, and then yelled. "Ella!"

She didn't answer. He looked all around him. He could see the cliff they'd jumped from behind him. The road lay beneath his feet, the asphalt hard and black. The ocean was still there. Everything was as it had been—

But he was all alone. He had the sense in that moment that he was the only person in this entire world.

And he started to feel panic rising inside of himself.

CHAPTER 11

Jazz had been alone before. When his dad had walked out, he had to walk the dog a couple of times before his mom got home from work, and sometimes that would be very late. He'd learned to fix dinner, and to start the gas grill in the back yard, and to get his homework done before she came home from the clinic. He liked helping, because his mom worked so hard, but it did get lonely, and a little creepy, at times.

Then she'd cut her hours back so she could be home by 5:00.

On a couple of occasions before that, he'd thought about inviting in his friends. He didn't like being in the house by himself. When he got really lonely, he thought it might be be fun to have some people over.

But then he'd realized that if he gave his mom a reason not to trust him, she'd have to hire a sitter to supervise him until she could get home. To be fair, he learned that from Ilsa, a high school girl who lived next door. Ilsa's mom was a flight attendant, and a couple of times a month she had to be out of town overnight. Some of the older kids in the neighborhood suggested—in fact, a couple of times had tried to get in—that she have parties when her mom was out of town.

"Why don't you?" he'd asked Ilsa, and she'd repeated what she'd said about how her mom, a single mother like Jazz's mom, would have to hire some one to come in to supervise her.

That would cost money, and take away from their budget, and mean no eating out with her mom, maybe no going to movies, and so she made the decision to be responsible.

Responsible, Jazz thought, trying to calm himself and think logically. "Is that what I'm supposed to learn here? All by myself?"

He remembered the amulet and held it up. Usually in this strange world that they'd come to, he could just step back into his own world—

No, he realized. I can't do that. I can't leave Ella here. What if something's happened to her? Still, he looked hard at the amulet—

And it didn't change. It stayed solid, not becoming a window as usual.

Okay, he said. I'll have to walk back and see if I can find Space Mountain by myself. He looked at the cliff.

I can't climb that, he thought. I'm not strong enough, It'll be dark by the time I get to the top—if I can get to the top.

If I can.

No. Don't say that. Remember what Yoda said in Star Wars: "Do. Or do not. There is no 'try.'" His favorite film: *The Empire Strikes Back*. Yeah. Do. Or do not.

He walked to the huge cliff. Do, he said to himself. I can do this.

Jazz saw a small ledge and climbed up to it. He swung his leg over the edge and rolled onto the ledge. Lying flat, he turned and started to look how far he'd come—

--And then changed his mind. No, He said to himself. Why would I care about what's down there? I need to focus on moving up. Not back to where I was. I'll look down when I get to the top, he decided.

He found handholds and pulled himself up foot by foot, and then yard by yard.

What seemed like a long time later he looked up. He still had a way to go, but not as far as when he started. He comforted himself with that knowledge. Don't look down, he told himself again.

Up he climbed again. He thought about the mountain climbing stories he'd read: he remembered reading about Sir Edmund Hillary and the conquest of Mount Everest. Hillary had to be scared, he reasoned, but he didn't quit. And when he arrived at the top, he had to climb back down. All I have to do is get to the top. Keep going.

His arms and legs were beginning to ache now. He remembered the cheers and acclaim that Hillary and Tensing, his Sherpa assistant, received all over the world, far and wide--

In that second Jazz realized that this situation was his test. He thought about one time that he'd been studying for a science test, and realized there was nothing to do but to memorize the material. It made him mad and resentful to have to do that.

Mom had knocked on his open door and saw him sitting on the bed. She came into the bedroom and asked, "What are you doing?"

"Memorizing," he replied sullenly. "I have a science test, and I hate memorizing, but I guess there's no way around it."

Mom sat on the bed. "I know," she said. "I guess the only comfort I can offer you is to tell you that I had to memorize entire text books when I was doing my studies at Medical School."

"I know," he said. "I don't look forward to that."

"One thing I can tell you," she said. "Memorization seems to be an acquired skill."

Jazz must have looked puzzled, for she seemed to be amused at his frustration. "I mean, it's something that the more you do it, the easier it becomes. Your skill in memorizing improves as you do it. You know Mr. Loggins at church?"

"Sure," he said.

"Well, he's assigned himself the task of memorizing the Bible."

"Memorizing the Bible?" The idea astounded Jazz. He couldn't imagine such a thing.

Mom nodded. "Lots of work, I know," she said. "But like he told me, 'Life is long. I might as well fill that time with something that interests me and makes me better as a person."

That was the key here. Yeah, he was scared, and alone. Yes, this seemed to be dangerous. But he realized as he climbed from rock to rock, from handhold to handhold, evaluating his route, that he could do this. He might be afraid, but this was something you'd expect in your life: sometimes, you'd face tasks that at first you'd think you couldn't do. But then you go ahead and try. If you could do it, you'd move your life along, and have an accomplishment accompanied by a real sense of pride.

Like Mom with medical school. When she started she was uncertain that she could do it. But she just kept going. Just keep going....Don't look down.

In what seemed like an hour he was within a few feet of the top. He looked to his left and realized that there probably would have been an easier route to the top. He looked to his right and saw the same thing. Too late for that, he thought.

"This is the route I chose and I have to finish it off. I can't start over again."

Another foot. Climb. Reset your feet. Pull up. Again. Again.

Then he could look over the top. He didn't see Ella yet, but still had a bit to go. Climb. Reset your feet. Pull. Again.

Then he reset his feet and swung his right leg over the top. He pulled himself up and swung his other leg over. Then he rolled once, twice, a third time—

He was safe.

It was over. He'd made it.

Jazz lay on his stomach, breathing hard. "I made it," he said to himself. "I climbed up that hill. I really did do it."

"Yes, you did," said a voice. "Good job."

He looked up.

A man stood in front of him. Well, he seemed to be a man. He was tall, and slim, and he glowed all over. His pure white hair was long and his eyes were a peculiar shade of yellow—

--No, not yellow. The eyes were golden. A pure, glowing, glorious gold, filled with love and approval.

He could see that the man—was he the Angel?—smiled with a profound attitude of pride. "You did it, Jazz," said the man, and took Jazz's hand. He gave a gentle tug and Jazz rose to his feet. The man pulled some more and Jazz walked with him away from the cliff's edge. In a matter of a few moments, they had moved far away from danger and toward what looked like a campfire.

"Ella!" he yelled. His friend looked up—he could see that she'd been crying and probably for quite a while, at that. Her cheeks stained with tears and her eyes were all red and puffy— and then she saw him.

"Jazz," she shouted, her voice hoarse. She jumped to her feet and ran to him, throwing her arms around him. "Oh Jazz, I was so worried about you. How did you get up that cliff?"

Jazz looked at the man who stood with his arm around his shoulders. "I—climbed," he stammered.

"You'll be fine now, Jasper," grinned the man. "I'll see you soon."

Then the man was gone. No rush of air, no sound effect, no glowing lights—just gone. Like someone had thrown a light switch.

Ella and Jazz continued to hug for a few moments. At last he pulled back and shouted, "I did it. I climbed up that cliff."

"Uh, huh, you did," she laughed.

"How did you get here?"

Ella paused. "Well—I don't know. I was walking with you, and we were talking, and suddenly, I was here, next to the fire. I got up and walked around, but I got a strong feeling that I should stay here and just wait."

"Who made the fire?" he asked.

"I don't know that either."

He looked at his hands. They were dirty and scraped, rather the worse for his climb. "Can we go back now?"

"Sure," she said. "Let's talk as we walk."

They both sensed the direction they were supposed to walk, and headed that way. Before a couple of minutes had elapsed, though, they found themselves at the entrance to Space Mountain and they walked in. After a few seconds, they found themselves on the ride again, and then they were swooping in to the final coasting. The attendants helped them out and they began to walk back to the entrance of Magic Kingdom.

CHAPTER 12

The monorail was mostly empty. They saw Space Mountain off to the north and east as the train started around. They remained silent as they pulled into the station in the Contemporary, and they saw lots of people waiting to board for their trip around.

Jazz and Ella entered the elevator and went up to their floor. Jazz used his wrist band to unlock and open the door.

The maid had not been there yet, and his mom was still asleep. They heard no sound from the other room either. Ella tiptoed to the door between the rooms and peeked in. "He's still asleep too," she whispered, as she turned back to her friend. "What do you want to do?"

"Let's leave a note and go down to breakfast," he suggested. She nodded and they went back to the elevator and down to the fourth floor. They went down to Chef Mickey's café area.

They picked up their breakfasts and sat down at a table for four, assuming their parents would soon be there. They ate in silence for several moments. "What happened to us today, Jazz?"

"I don't know for sure," said Jazz. "I just suddenly stood there all by myself."

She understood his bewilderment.

"Then I looked all around for you," he said. "When I

couldn't find you, I began to climb."

She shuddered. "Do you hate heights too?"

"Well, no, but it was still very scary," he said. "I just told myself to keep climbing."

"That's what you have to learn, then," she said. "Don't quit. Just keep climbing."

"I keep thinking of the fish in *Finding Nemo*," he said. "Remember that silly fish that travels with the father fish?"

"Sure," she smiled at the memory of Dory, the forgetful fish. "Ellen DeGeneres."

"Right," he said. "Anyway, she said that her motto was 'Just keep swimming, just keep swimming, swimming, swimming, swimming.'"

Ella laughed out loud. "Yes, I loved that," she said. "She was my favorite fish."

"I know," he said. "But I kept chanting that to myself: 'just keep climbing, just keep climbing.'"

They chuckled together.

"I guess that's the lesson," he said. "Don't give up. Keep going."

"Maybe you've got your motto for your life," she suggested. "I heard that Davy Crockett's life motto was 'Be sure you're right, then go ahead.'"

"Yeah," he said, "but he died at the Alamo."

"Yeah," she said, almost mocking him. "But he made his decision and stuck with it, and never gave up. You could have died on the side of that mountain, Jazz. If you'd made a misstep, or slipped, you could have fallen and died."

"I guess," he shrugged.

"Why did you do it? Why take the chance?"

He considered. "I guess it was because I couldn't figure out how else to get home and...uh..."

"To find me?" she asked. "To save me?"

His face reddened. He grew embarrassed. "Yeah," he said. "You're worth it."

"Thank you," she said.

He nodded. "Would you have done the same for me?"

"Not a chance," she said. He started for a second, and then saw the teasing grin on her face.

"Yes, you would," he said, mocking her.

At that moment their parents joined them. "Based on the note you left, you two must have been up early," said Mr. Butler.

"Trouble sleeping, I guess," said Ella. "We've even been on Space Mountain already." Both parents looked surprised.

"I didn't hear you even go out," Jazz's mom said.

"You must really love that ride," he said. The two teenagers shared a secret look.

The talk turned to the wedding , and the rehearsal dinner, which was going to be held that night. They'd have a rehearsal at 5:00 that afternoon and then come back for dinner at the Grand Floridian. Ella and Jazz nodded their understanding of the days' events.

"I have to go the Airport in a few minutes," said Dad. "Do you guys want to come?"

"Sure," said Ella. "Why, though?"

"Well, a few people are coming in for our wedding," he said. "Like Jazz's Grandma and Grandpa, and your grandparents, too, Ella" he explained. Jazz and Ella were thrilled at the prospect of seeing their grandparents.

CHAPTER 13

The grandparents were delighted their grandchildren had come to greet them at the airport, and the drive back to the Contemporary was filled with nonstop chattering and anticipation of the evening ahead. Jazz and Ella helped their grandparents get settled in their rooms at the Contemporary, and then took them on the monorail for a visit to Epcot.

"Should we go on Spaceship Earth?" asked Jazz.

"I don't know," said Ella. "We don't have any further instructions, do we? I mean, what to do next?"

He admitted they didn't but said, "Maybe we'll learn something there. Or somewhere else."

The group exited the monorail and made their way into the park. Jazz found that he liked Ella's Gramma and Grampa a great deal, and she obviously enjoyed his grandparents as well.

As they entered the park, everyone steered toward Spaceship Earth and stood in line. It took some time, but the line kept moving, and soon the all family members were entering the area where people were being loaded on the ride. Ella turned to Jazz, "Let's ride with our grandparents, okay?"

"Yeah," he said, appreciating the idea. "Okay, maybe then nothing out of the ordinary will happen."

It was a snug fit, but the ride moved upwards at the same

leisurely pace as always. Their grandparents had never been to Epcot and told the kids how impressed they were—

And then everything froze. "Ella," said Jazz.

"Yes," said Ella.

"We're supposed to get off here, aren't we?"

"I think so, yes," she agreed.

The restraining bars slid forward and the two friends climbed out. Once again the figure of Thucydides came over to them. "Come," he said. "We need you. You are ready."

He held out his hands and helped them onto the stage. "Go through that portal," he said, indicating a door at the back of the set. "Be careful. You must come back."

"Mr. Thucydides," said Jazz. "Why us?"

"Yes," said Ella. "Why would you pick us?"

"Because you have been burdened with two of the heaviest losses that people your age can face," he said. "You, Jazz, have been betrayed by a parent and you have been forced to live without a father. Ella, you had to learn to deal with death long before you should have."

"Is there more?" said Ella.

"Yes, something else," he said. "You have shown yourselves to have extraordinary character and wisdom. You, Ella, jumped feet first into your greatest fear, which was the fear of heights. You, Jazz, had to climb out of a desperate situation. You both responded as we had hoped.

"What do you mean?", questioned Ella.

Thucydides embraced them. "You will understand more when you return," he said. "Just be brave for now and know that the forces of Good stand behind you."

He put his hands on their heads and gave them a blessing.

"Then go, young friends. I hope someday people remember what you have done."

Jazz and Ella, both confused, obeyed and walked forward. "Each of you take a torch," said one of the students, who stood beside the portal. He handed Ella a torch, and then gave one to Jazz. "Be brave. You will be walking into darkness," the student said. They took the torches.

Ella turned to him. "What do you think?" she asked.

"I can't imagine what this is about," he said.

She reached for him and gave him a brief hug. "I know," she said. "Let's just press ahead."

Jazz nodded. She took his hand and they walked through the portal.

CHAPTER 14

It was, as Thucydides' student had warned them, black as molasses. The torches had a hard time penetrating the darkness as they moved ahead, but at least the ground seemed to be smooth.

"Be careful, Jazz," Ella reminded him.

They saw what looked like a living room. The furniture was shabby and the rug worn and with holes. A huge television set hung on the wall. They walked into the room.

A man sat in a chair with a pop top can in his hand. He was dressed in shabby clothes and had propped his feet on a coffee table in front of him. He didn't look up as the teen-agers walked over to him.

"Do you know us?" asked Jazz.

He didn't look up. "Naw," he sneered.

"What are you watching?" Ella asked.

"An infomercial," he said.

"For what?" asked Jazz.

"I dunno," he said. "Some gadget. You use it peel oranges, I think. Sumpin like that."

Ella looked at Jazz and they began to circle the room. They saw no books, no art work, no musical instruments, no chess sets, just a couple of lamps.

Dirty. That was the word. The best word to describe it.

"Do you live here, sir?" asked Ella.

The man didn't look up. "Yeah."

"Do you have any books?" asked Jazz.

Now he did look up. "Wha' for?"

"Do you read?" asked Ella.

"No," said the man. "No, I hate reading."

The two teenagers looked at one another.

"I know what this is, I think," said Jazz. "

"Me, too," said Ella. "Sloth. I mean, laziness."

"Right," said Jazz. "Do you think he's real?"

"No," she said. "At least, not real as we understand it. He's a personification, I think."

"A what?"

"It means he's a symbol of something," said Ella. "He stands for those who are defeated by life and can't get their lives going."

"Come on," he said.

They walked several yards down the path with the torchlight and found another room. It was familiar this time. Three boys—Albert, Bill, and Frankie, Jazz realized—sat there with snide expressions on their faces, making fun of a smaller boy. "It's me," said Jazz. "They're tormenting me."

"What are we seeing, really?" asked Ella.

In a flash, Jazz understood. "It's another one of the Seven Deadly Sins," said Jazz. "I get it. I studied this in school last year. I think we're going to see all the seven deadly sins."

"Which one is this?"

"I think it could be murder," said Jazz.

"No," said Ella. "It can't be. No one died."

He thought for a second. "Yes. We just can't see it here. A lot of me died at their hands."

Ella nodded her understanding. "You think there's more than one type of murder, then."

"I'm starting to think so," he said. "But their cruelty is something that I can undo."

"How?"

He thought. "I can refuse to give them any power over me," he said. "I can kill what they did to me."

She smiled. "Don't let them have the ability to destroy you."

"Easier said than done," he replied.

"Yes?" she said. "Have they ever walked into the dark like you to make something right?"

"I doubt it."

"No, of course not," said Ella. "Bullies are cowards. Don't let them have you."

They walked on. Their torches illuminated two girls sitting together. One of them was crying and one of them was...

"Me?" said Ella.

"Who is that?"

"She used to be my best friend," said Ella.

"Used to be?"

"Yeah," said Ella. "Watch what happened."

The Ella in the vision spoke. "You voted against me in cheerleading tryouts?"

"Yes," said the other girl, and cried harder.

"Why?"

"Oh you always get everything you want," said the girl. "Everything. It comes to you so easy."

Vision Ella said, "No. It doesn't. I worked for hours and hours on those flips. I practiced and practiced. Did you think I just went out there and did it?"

"I know that's just what you did," said the girl. "You think you're so great. So smart. Always…" The vision faded.

"Another one of the Seven Deadly Sins," said Ella. "This time directed at me."

"Right," said Jazz. "The sin of Envy."

"So that's why she didn't want to be friends with me anymore?" asked Ella.

"Is that what happened?" asked Jazz. "She dumped you?"

"Yes," said Ella. "We haven't spoken since."

Jazz and Ella walked into the dark. She took his arm. "She voted against me," she said. "Her name is Angela. She wanted to be in the 'popular group' at the junior high. So she sat with the other girls and voted against me. She didn't speak up for me."

"So is she in the 'popular' group now?" asked Jazz.

"I suppose."

"So did you find another group of friends?" asked Jazz. His stomach churned, thinking about his friend Ella and the pain she must have been in.

"I found you," she said. "You and I are pals, aren't we?"

He grinned and started to respond, but another tableau presented itself. They saw and responded to lust, greed, wrath, and lastly pride.

A man sat waiting for them as they completed pride. He stood and appeared to be golden, and they recognized the man who had visited them on several occasions.

"Sir," said Ella. "What do we have to do next?"

He looked puzzled. "What do you mean?" he asked.

"We've seen all these lessons," said Ella. "Things we really have to avoid, isn't that true?"

He tilted his head to one side. "Not exactly," he said. "Those were called the Seven Deadly Sins by the ancients, and they are listed and explained in many books of wisdom. I brought you here because they are part of you, too."

"I get angry," said Jazz. "But I don't think that's the same as Wrath as a deadly sin, is it?"

"Why do you think the boys bullied you in the library at the public school?" asked the Man.

Jazz thought. "Because they didn't like me," he said. "They wouldn't do that to someone they like, or admire."

"Not exactly," said the Man. "They attacked you because they are so inferior to others in their own minds that they came after you, to ease their own sense of personal inferiority."

"Are they inferior to me, you mean?" asked Jazz.

"In their relentless attack on you, their teasing—the one even spat in your face, didn't he?—was intended to bolster their own childish vanity. They didn't like someone like you: intelligent, a good athlete, with a fine family."

"Don't they have families, Sir?" asked Jazz.

"Yes," he said. "But they are not the same as yours. They do not feel love, they do not feel joy in the home, and so they retaliate on someone like yourself."

"But I'm just another boy," Jazz said.

"Not to them," He said. "You were smaller than they, vulnerable, and afraid of them. Cowards always attack those who fear them. But do not worry. You will not see them again."

"What about those other girls?" asked Ella.

The Man sighed. "All your life, you will deal with those who feel inferior to you in some way. In this case, girls who didn't have the courage or the determination to pursue excellence, and to pay the price for it, betrayed you. They saw you as a threat. If you succeeded, they would have a mark to which they had to raise themselves. You would stand out on the Cheerleading squad unless they worked as hard as you did. Were they lacking the talent? No, they could have done as well as you. They could have paid the price you did. But that would mean hours of hard work, as you know. They were not willing to pay the price."

"Is that Sloth?" asked Jazz, since Ella was still crying.

"Yes," said the man. "But you also had to deal with their Wrath, with their Envy, and their Pride. They couldn't face the challenge to their own pride."

"Being excellent has a price," said Jazz, putting an arm around his friend.

"If you were to name the best basketball player of all time," said the Man, "I think you'd probably name Michael Jordan. A lot of people, however, don't know that he didn't make his high school team when he was a sophomore."

"Michael Jordan?" exclaimed Jazz.

"Yes," said the Man. "But he paid the price. When he was a professional, he would arrive at the Chicago stadium at four o'clock in the afternoon. Then he would shoot, and shoot, and shoot some more. Next he would spend a long time dribbling the ball. He'd then shoot baskets in all sorts of positions, from all over the court. The reason he was so deadly was that he practiced so diligently, and took complete advantage of his great natural ability and his physical strength and mental toughness."

Ella spoke up. "So we are being prepared for something, Sir?"

"I think you're ready," smiled the man, and he disappeared.

Suddenly they were back in the cars at Spaceship Earth. Ella sat between her grandmother and grandfather, and Jazz sat between his grandparents. The ride ended and the two teenagers walked out of Spaceship Earth with their families. "Now what?" asked Ella, whispering in Jazz's ear.

"I think we have to wait," he said. "We weren't given any assignment, were we?"

"No," said Ella. "At least, not directly." She looked at him and a tear started down her cheek. "I'm getting tired of all this, not knowing what to expect next," she said.

"I know," he said. "Why don't we focus on the wedding and rehearsal and reception and all that? Have some fun?"

"Good idea," she said, and wiped the tear from her eyes. "That's what we'll do," she added.

What he did next seemed perfect to both of them. He reached for her and gave her a bear hug. "Look, we have each other to lean on, right?"

"Yeah," she said.

"What if we sneak over there after the wedding?"

"Okay," she said. "I'm willing, sure."

The rehearsal went well, and was over in less than ten minutes. The group of grandparents, parents and two teenagers dined at the remarkably expensive Victoria and Albert's Restaurant in the Grand Floridian Hotel.

"I've never seen a menu like this," said Jazz to Ella. "I don't even know what most of this stuff is." The waiter appeared, and suggested Jazz order Dungeness & King Crab served with spring asparagus and Calvisius caviar. Ella ordered an appetizer of Smoked Colorado Buffalo Tenderloin served with braised fennel, radishes, and Satsuma tangerine vinaigrette. For dinner, they each ordered Australian "Kobe" Beef Tenderloin with smoked garlic potato puree since they both recognized the terms 'potato' and 'beef tenderloin'. Dessert for Jazz was Hawaiian Kona Chocolate Souffle. Ella and her dad split a Pyramid of Tanzanie Dark Chocolate Mousse, which, their waiter told them, was inspired by the "Year of a Million Dreams." No one was disappointed with their dinner that night.

CHAPTER 15

When the two families met in the hallway to go to the wedding chapel, Ella was wearing the beautiful new dress that her mother-to-be had bought for her, and took her father's arm. Jazz looked handsome in his rented tuxedo as his mother took his arm and let him escort her to the elevator.

They had to wait a few moments for the monorail, and Jazz had a chance to talk to his friend. "Did we get a new project?" he asked.

"Not that I know," she said. He could see that Ella again had to struggle not to cry.

"Why are you so sad?" he asked.

"I keep thinking of my real mom," she said.

"Yeah," he said.

"I mean, your mom is great, and I know she'll be good to me, and..." she trailed off.

"I like your dad too," he said. "And I guess you're—uh—okay—"

Ella, knowing he was teasing, poked him in the stomach. "Shut up," she laughed. "You have no idea how lucky you are", she replied, teasing him back.

"Look, I think things will work out, don't you?" he asked, trying to be serious.

"I know they will," she said. "It will be great to have a mom, and a brother, and a family. Our parents will love us, I'm sure, and it's going to be great."

"Is something else bothering you?", He asked.

"We haven't been doing this stuff for no reason, I mean, seeing these visions, climbing cliffs and jumping off them," she said. "Someone wants us to learn something."

He thought. "Do you think it would help to go back on Space Mountain?"

"Hmm," she said, considering. "Well, not tonight because of the wedding stuff."

"Of course," he said.

"How about Saturday morning?" she asked. "Everyone will be sound asleep when the park opens. We can get over there early."

He thought about it, and decided she had a good plan. "One thing's for sure," he said. "We have to do it. If nothing else, we've learned to go right at things that scare us."

"Okay," she agreed, "we'll face it with the courage we've been learning."

"Most people don't ever learn that except by experience," said Jazz. "I think we've been blessed. Many people miss out on a lot because they're scared to go ahead and try something they ought to, like your dad and that quarterback experience."

CHAPTER 16

The wedding would become one of their all-time favorite memories. The beautiful pavilion was decked out with a bountiful amount of gorgeous, sweet smelling white roses, gardenias, and lilies. Ella preceded Jazz and his mom down a short aisle, carrying a bouquet of delicate pink and white roses. Mom, holding on to Jazz's arm, carried a bouquet of Calla lilies. Ella stood next to her dad during the ceremony and Jazz next to his mother as two separate families joined together.

Both Ella and Mom cried, as well as both of the grandmothers who were so touched that their children had found such happiness again. Jazz couldn't stop smiling during the brief ceremony. After the wedding, the new family had a small reception at the Polynesian Hotel, and after dinner returned to the Contemporary Hotel.

The parents had arranged for the grandparents to keep an eye on the two teenagers and drove off for a weekend honeymoon in Daytona Beach. Jazz and Ella ate a light dinner with their grandparents at Chef Mickey's in the Contemporary Hotel, then went to bed at about ten, chatting well into the night about what their new life together as brother and sister would be like before falling asleep.

The phone rang at 6:30 a. m. from the wake-up call and the

two teenagers changed into jeans and ran to the monorail. At the Magic Kingdom, they rushed around to Space Mountain. The ride zoomed and careened as always, but at about halfway into the ride, everything changed again.

"Where are we this time?" asked Jazz.

"I think we're on Spaceship Earth," said Ella. Sure enough, they had been transported into the ride and were climbing into the tableau.

But this wasn't exactly Spaceship Earth. The ride was the same, the cars were the same, and the same narrator was speaking.

But he wasn't speaking the same script that Jazz and Ella had heard a few times before.

"Here are scenes from the future," said the Narrator. "They are going to show you what could be coming, Ella and Jazz."

"Could be coming?" said Jazz. "So these things aren't set in stone."

"No, I don't have that feeling," said Ella.

"Here is your first Homecoming dance," said the Narrator. "As you can see, Ella is going with another boy, and you aren't going at all, Jazz."

Ella stood in the center of the living room. She had her long hair done up on top of her head, and wore an Emerald green gown that made her eyes sparkle.

"You look beautiful," said Jazz, a bit weakly.

"Thank you," said Ella.

Now they saw a Jazz figure, standing in the hallway, watching as a tall junior boy gave Ella a wrist corsage of tiny roses. She leaned up and hugged him, and Mom and Dad stood by beaming.

"I feel sick," said Jazz.

Ella turned to him. "Why didn't you ask me?"

"I don't know."

The wagon moved past the tableau and another one came in sight. "It's me," he said. Indeed, Jazz stood wearing a dirty football uniform, outfitted with all the pads and wearing cleats on his feet. He was holding a helmet and looked exhausted, but happy. A cheerleader stood opposite him. She was saying, "Oh Jazz, you were terrific." She took his arm and began walking with him.

"Uh…thanks," he said. The girl was attractive, taller than Ella, and had a sensational smile.

"We're going to be conference champs," said the girl. "We're also going to the playoffs…"

Now Jazz and Ella saw an Ella figure in the background. She wore a cheerleading uniform and looked very upset.

"You're the varsity quarterback," Ella in the car said to Jazz, next to her.

"I am?" he said. He found himself smiling. "Well, you're a cheerleader. I bet you're the best one."

"That girl is after you to be her boyfriend," she said.

Jazz understood. "She also is jealous of you," he said. "Not because of me, though."

"Because of who I am?" whispered Ella.

The car moved to the next tableau. Now the two friends stood in front of several crates and suitcases. The Ella figure said, "So I guess this is goodbye," as she bit her lower lip.

"Yeah," the Jazz figure said. "Mom and Dad are waiting to take you to the airport. You'd better hurry."

"Well, I'll see you at Christmas, right?" she said, and a tear ran down her cheek.

"Okay," he said. "I...I'll miss you. Tear 'em up at Dartmouth, right?"

"Yeah," she managed a smile. "You do the same at Stanford." She turned and started out of the tableau.

"We're going to different Universities," said Ella in the cart.

"Uh, huh," said Jazz. "On opposite sides of the country."

The tableau shifted and another came into view. Now, Jazz saw himself standing at the altar in a large church. He was wearing a formal tuxedo with a carnation in his lapel. Several men stood next to him, and he realized it was his wedding party. He looked to the right and saw several young women dressed in bridesmaid's gowns.

The Jazz in the cart looked at the tableau and saw the bride coming down the aisle. A man was next to her, and she held his arm. But it wasn't Ella's dad. Now the girl stood next to him. He looked at her.

Even through the veil, he could see that it wasn't Ella. He'd never seen this girl before.

"Who is she?" asked Ella, watching the tableau next to him in the cart.

"I don't know," he said. "Not a clue."

"She is very beautiful," managed Ella. Jazz turned and saw that she was weeping.

Now the tableau shifted. Ella saw a much older Ella standing outside a hospital. Jazz walked up to her and gave her a hug. "Norm's gone, then," he said, "I'm so sorry."

Ella in the cart said, "I think my future husband just died."

"Yeah," said Jazz in the cart, and saw that the Jazz in the tableau was all by himself also.

Jazz in the tableau said, "It'll be okay, Ella. We can take care of each other."

Another tableau came into view. It was a graveyard—

"No!" screamed Ella in the cart.

"Don't show us!" said Jazz, next to her---

--And they found themselves back on the Space Mountain Ride, careening, shooting up and down. In moments, the ride coasted in to the platform, where Jazz and Ella exited. They walked into the bright sunlight, neither one of them speaking, shaken by seeing the future.

"Was it really the future?" asked Jazz.

"I don't know," said Ella. She took his arm. "I didn't like it, if it was."

"But nothing really happened—I mean, it isn't for sure that it will happen like that, is it?"

They sat side by side at a table near an ice cream stand. Neither felt like talking. "Are you sad?" he asked.

She didn't answer for a few moments. "I don't know," she said. "Why do you think we were shown that?"

A man sat down across the table from them with an ice cream bar. The two teenagers saw that the bar had ears, like a Mickey Mouse hat, and they smiled. "Here," said the man. He handed them each an ice cream bar and said, "Enjoy them. You've earned them."

Now they recognized him. It was the same man who'd been showing them the tasks that they had to perform.

They unwrapped the ice cream bars and ate for a few moments. They found themselves calming down and regaining some composure.

"Were those scenes real representations of the future?"

asked Jazz, afraid of what the man would say.

"Yes, maybe," said the man.

"Maybe?" asked Ella.

"Yes," said the man. "Think of them as—unwritten novels, maybe."

"What does that mean?" asked Ella.

"It mean that your futures haven't been written," he said. "You have choices. You always have choices."

"Will we live out our lives like that?" asked Jazz.

"You could," said the man. "You could hurt each other. You could also love each other. You could decide if you want to be those people you saw or if you want something else."

"You mean we…can do what we want?" asked Ella.

"Yes," said the man. "You don't have to be bound by what you saw in the tableaus. Those were just 'possible' outcomes."

"We have choices, don't we?" said Jazz.

"Jazz, why did your father leave your family?" asked the Man.

Jazz thought. "He—made a choice, didn't he."

"Exactly right," the man said. "Instead of learning to live with your mother, to make changes in himself, to ask her to change, he indulged himself in things he should not have."

"I think I understand," said Jazz, his voice almost a whisper.

"Dear Ella," said the man. "Can you talk about your mother?"

"I think so," she said, but her voice was shaky.

"Why did she die?" asked the Man.

"I dunno," she said.

"Yes, you do," said the man. "You may not like it, but you do know."

"She smoked," Ella said.

"She did not smoke when she was getting ready to be your mother," said the Man. "She put aside the habit but then went back to it a few years later."

"She also ate a terrible diet," Ella went on. "Sweets; Ice cream and desserts; she ate a bag of potato chips everyday."

"Also liquor," said the Man.

Ella nodded. "She drank way too much."

"And why did she do these things?"

Ella shrugged. "There is only one reason someone takes up smoking," said the Man.

"You mean peer pressure?" asked Jazz. "She felt she had to keep up with what her friends were doing?"

The Man shook his head. "For someone to decide to smoke because others force them to do so," he said, "is a myth. People smoke, or drink, or use dangerous drugs, because they *want* to."

Jazz thought about this. "So they make a decision," he said. "In order to smoke, you have to decide to smoke."

"Yes," said the man. "It is a fairly easy addiction to acquire. It requires much more strength to rid yourself of the habit once it is acquired."

"But why would someone want to smoke then?" asked Jazz. "Why would they want to? It smells bad, it isn't really enjoyed by others—"

"No," agreed the Man. "People, without variation, start to smoke because they want to feel accepted. They believe that this habit will give them the ability to operate on a level field with people who they believe are somehow better than they are."

"All smokers don't like themselves?" asked Ella.

The Man nodded. "It is a little more complicated than that,

but they certainly don't feel confident enough about themselves to say "no" when others are encouraging them to follow the crowd. It's very much the same with harmful drugs," he said. "Both habits require a decision and a commitment to that decision."

"So we don't have to smoke," said Ella.

"Nor use drugs, nor drink to excess," said the Man. "You can decide not to do things which harm you. No one will actually force you."

Ella looked up. "That was the purpose of the tableaus about us being treated so badly."

"Of course," said the Man.

"May I ask a question?" asked Jazz.

"Of course again," said the Man, smiling.

"Will Ella and I spend our lives together?"

Ella smiled, and the smile seemed to Jazz like the dawn after a long cold night. Her face was radiant. She took his arm and squeezed it in a hug.

"Dear ones," said the Man. "Everything you saw today is a choice. You can decide to be together. You can also decide to remain the very best of friends. You can also decide to see each other never again in your lives, once you leave home."

Ella squeezed Jazz' arm. "That will be a decision, won't it?" she asked. "We can decide to get along, and be kind to one another, or we can live in misery, isn't that true?"

"Yes," said the man. "I think you need to go back to the Hotel and take your Grandparents to breakfast."

And then he wasn't there.

"Where did he go?" asked Jazz.

"He went back to where he came from," smiled Ella. "He'll

keep an eye on us."

"Are we going to be okay?"

"That depends," said Ella.

"On what?" asked Jazz.

"On the decisions we make," said his best friend. "We've been charged to make good ones."

"Right," said Jazz. "I think you're right. No, I know you are right."

CHAPTER 17
Six Months Later

Jazz adjusted his hat, pulling the brim down to just above his eyes. "Do I look okay?"

"Better than okay," said his mother, grinning at him. "You look terrific."

"You bet," said his stepfather, looking up from his coffee. "You got football practice tonight?"

"Yeah," said Jazz. "It's just a walk-through, though. We've got our first game Saturday, you know."

"We do," teased his mother and step-father. "Yeah, you've reminded us many times," said Mom. "You are starting, right?"

"He's the quarterback, Mom," said his step-sister. "He's going to be terrific."

"Okay, hustle, you're going to miss your buses," said Dad.

Jazz and Ella walked out the front door, headed toward their respective bus stops. "Let me put you on the spot," said Ella, grinning.

"Sure," said Jazz, smiling at his step-sister.

"Are you happy that you decided to go to Marmion?" she asked.

"Yeah," he said. "I never thought I'd like a military school, which it is—"

"Like I didn't know that," she sneered.

"—Yeah, sorry," he said. "I think I needed the personal discipline involved in a Military High School. They're teaching me some pretty good stuff, not just in the classes or on the team. Yeah, I guess it's a little strict, but…"

"And you like football," she nodded.

"Yeah, the guys are great," he said. "Coach is tough, but he does make it fun, you know."

"Uh, huh," she said, grinning up at her step brother and best friend.

"How do you like the high school?" he asked.

"It's going well, so far," she said. "My classes are interesting, too. I really like my English teacher. We're going to read *Great Expectations*, by Dickens—"

"Right," he nodded.

"And I like my classes fine."

"Great," he said.

"How are you doing?" she asked.

"Okay," he said. "It is kind of strange not having girls in my classes, but it's okay. My classes are pretty interesting, too."

"Mom did talk to me last summer about Rosary, you know, the girl's school—"

"Uh-huh," said Jazz.

"But I had decided to go to the public high school for at least a year," she said. "I made the decision and I'm going to stick with it."

"Well, that's what they asked us to do," agreed Jazz. "Make a decision and stick with it. We can evaluate next summer."

"I'm trying out for cheerleading tonight, Jazz."

"Great," he said. "You'll do great."

"You think so?"

"No," he said, "I know so."

Stepbrother and stepsister continued walking and talking until they reached the bus stop. When their buses came, they went off into their separate worlds.

But they would come together again.

THE END

Title: ACID

- Author: Jeff Lovell
- Publisher: TotalRecall Publications, Inc.
- HARD COVER ISBN: 978-1-59095-116-3
- PAPERBACK, ISBN: 978-1-59095-117-0
- EBOOK, Nook, Kindle, ISBN: 978-1-59095-118-7
- Number of pages: 352
- Publication Date: 2013

Rick Howell, living in the shadow of two women who have the power to change reality, must risk his life to stop the genocidal exploits of a desperate lunatic who wants to acquire their powers. The discovery of a mind controlling drug opens a pathway to frightening mental abilities for Rachel Farrell, who can move backward and forward in time at will, while Donna Riske, Rachel's best friend, can control the thoughts of others.

Title: The Coven of the Spring

- Author: Jeff Lovell
- Publisher: TotalRecall Publications, Inc.
- HARD COVER ISBN: 978-1-59095-113-2
- PAPERBACK, ISBN: 978-1-59095-114-9
- EBOOK, Nook, Kindle, ISBN: 978-1-59095-115-6
- Number of pages: 336
- Publication Date: 2013

An ancient secret, with frightening new powers, emerges to terrify and destroy.

Grace DeRosa, a gifted research chemist, lives with her husband Jim and their seventeen year old daughter Crissy. Grace finds a hidden spring in the woods near Salem, Massachusetts. She discovers that the consumed water imparts unique and fearful powers that lead to the ability to read minds, create terrifying mental pictures and force the user's will on others.

Title: Emerald

- Author: Jeff Lovell
- Publisher: TotalRecall Publications, Inc.
- HARD COVER ISBN: 978-1-59095-080-7
- PAPERBACK, ISBN: 978-1-59095-081-4
- EBOOK, Nook, Kindle, ISBN: 978-1-59095-082-1
- Number of pages: 348
- Publication Date: 2015

Emerald begins with a pirate assault on a merchant vessel. Blackbeard, or Edward Teach, terrorized the east coast of America from Nova Scotia down to the Virgin Islands. This book shows how people with a unique mental power called the Knack fight against the evil of pirates from 1715 to the present day, and even includes a long look at the court of King Arthur, and his chief advisor Myrthynne, who also had the most powerful manifestation of the Knack. This book, then, flows in several time periods and pulls together romance, villainy and a dramatic treasure, all of which frame a love story between a woman with the Knack and a man devoted to loving and protecting her.

Praise For Jim Nesbitt's Latest Work, *The Fatal Saving Grace: An Ed Earl Burch Novel*

"In *The Fatal Saving Grace*, Nesbitt delivers a scorched-earth tale set under the vast dome of West Texas sky, where every shadow conceals an ambush and every road bleeds history. Dark, relentless and steeped in the sweat and dust of border country, Jim Nesbitt writes with the authenticity of a man who has walked these roads, smelled that dry wind, and lived to tell the tale. The writing is hard-bitten but lyrical, equal parts gunpowder and poetry, capturing a land where men live by codes written in blood. Ed Earl Burch is one of the great contemporary hard-boiled protagonists—scarred, unyielding, and bound to his own brutal sense of right and wrong. Nesbitt paints Texas in colors of rust, smoke, and whiskey, and the result is a story that feels carved in stone. This is cowboy noir at its finest."

> **—Baron Birtcher,** Will Rogers Medallion winning author of *Knife River*

"Jim Nesbitt knows his Texas crime and writes one fine line at a time. Hard-boiled with prickly pears, old leather boots, a bit of tobacco, freshly spit of course, he gets it right."

> **—Joe R. Lansdale**, champion mojo storyteller and author of the Hap 'N Leonard crime thrillers

"A gritty and deadly must-read, THE FATAL SAVING GRACE cements Nesbitt's standing among the best writers in the pantheon of Southern noir."

> **—Bruce Robert Coffin,** bestselling author of the Detective Justice Mysteries

"Jim's beat-up, badass Dallas PI, an ex-cop named Ed Earl Burch who's partial to Duke Wayne and Jimmie Dale Gilmore, Lucky Strikes and Maker's Mark, makes Mike Hammer look like Miss Marple. Definitely not for the faint of heart, Jim's novels nonetheless offer wicked humor and a keen eye for the details of Texas terrain as well as brass-knuck action and language that would strip the paint off a Hummer."

    —**Noel Holston**, author of *Life After Deaf* and *As I Die Laughing*

"From the start, Jim Nesbitt comes in hot with *The Fatal Saving Grace* and delivers a scorcher from the first page to the last in his fifth Ed Earl Burch crime thriller. Ed Earl is pursued by a maniac of a killer seeking revenge in the badlands of West Texas. But Ed Earl, being the big-gun-wielding sumbitch he is, turns from hunted to hunter. He operates in a harsh yet stunning landscape, with its gun runners, drug mules and white supremacist hideouts. The borderland is a character in this story as much as any of the people. It is a place where evil wins too often, and the line between hero and villain is like an old, half-covered trail in the desert. Ed Earl isn't sure which side he wants to be on. But like West Texas itself, he is unforgiving—in his case, of those who come after him and his own. *The Fatal Saving Grace* is excellent cowboy noir that will carry thriller readers into a dark and violent world. They'll be very glad Ed Earl Burch is the one out front doing the gunslinging."

    —**Rich Zahradnik**, author of *The Bone Records* and *Lights Out Summer,* winner of the 2018 Shamus Award

"Nesbitt's descriptions of the grays, reds and blue blacks of the vast Texas southwest scenery is breathtaking. You see what those who live there see. Descriptions so captivating they become another character. Each disheveled, airless trailer, each windblown barn, each rusting truck-filled yard surrounded by rust-colored fencing is so evocative you imagine you were there once. Likewise the human centipedes, scorpions and rattlers have personalities all their own. Nobody gets a break. Fat, vengeful, or ruthless, no matter which side, what trait, all are called what they are. After a while, you wonder what keeps people chasing one another through this bleak, wind-whipped place where hope seems to go and die."

—**John William Davis**, author of *Rainy Street Stories* and *Around the Corner*

"Ed Earl Burch is the last guy you want to aggravate, even a little bit. It could be the last thing you ever do. With the first sentence of Jim Nesbitt's new cop thriller, *The Fatal Saving Grace*, you know where this journey is headed. People who deserve hurt will feel pain. Burch is a very human former cop turned private dick, now turning back to (legal) law enforcement and realizing the inherent trade-offs. He is crusty, savvy and profane. He's old and creaky and unimaginably tough. His reputation is well earned. And the scars are everywhere. Burch's code may not be the same as yours or mine, but it is ironclad. He will protect those who need it. And he's come to realize that his loyalty means as much to him as to others. This is powerful stuff. The action is hard and quick. And often final. Burch is besieged by drug dealers and stone-cold killers and corrupt lawmen, amid an often-reverent view of the high desert that has left its mark on this old cowboy. Nesbitt clearly loves the West, and, in his world, it is an ancient and very real place that will not leave its inhabitants unscathed. There is smoke and guns and whisky and women. And a world full of payback. Some of the words are soft and they paint a picture. "*Slow-moving ceiling fans stirred the dust motes floating through* the feeble rays of single-bulb lamps mounted high in each corner of the room and the harsher illumination sputtering from a rust-scaled fluorescent fixture over the bar." And sometimes they are "as comfortably lethal as asbestos wrapped around a steam pipe."

Burch will survive, although how he manages it is sometimes as much luck as it is his belligerent tenacity. Ed Earl Burch will not go quietly into that good night. This old lawman stays loud and proud."

  —**Michael Ludden**, author of *Alfredo's Luck, Tate Drawdy* and *The Street King*

"Ed Earl Burch is back, and that's great news for readers who love classic hard-boiled noir, colorful characters, crackling dialogue and plenty of action. You get all that—and a whole lot more—in THE FATAL SAVING GRACE (great title!), the fifth book in Jim Nesbitt's award-winning series about a battered, boozing but tough-as-nails lawman who is willing to break the law himself to get the job done. Ed Earl almost gets killed at the beginning here—and then the bodies pile up quickly as he goes on a harrowing, bloody journey to seek revenge and to see justice done. Despite all the violence, some of the scenes are laugh out loud funny too—like when Ed Earl casually asks his cop partner "excessive?" after brutally beating a bad guy to a pulp. All the pages of this winning action thriller just fly by with snappy, smart stuff from Nesbitt who clearly loves to write the Ed Earl Burch character as much as we love to read about him. So go grab yourself some Ed Earl Burch—this one, plus the earlier books, if you haven't read them yet. Highly recommended!"

  —**R.G. Belsky**, author of the Gil Malloy and Clare Carlson mysteries